THE WATERS OF MANILA BAY ARE NEVER SILENT

I.S.A. Crisostomo-Lopez is a writer based in Binan City, Philippines. She earned her Bachelor's degree in Communication Arts from the University of the Philippines Los Baños in 1996 and her Master's degree in Creative Writing from De La Salle University Manila in 2003. She is married with four children.

She has published several works of fiction including 'Passage', which was anthologized in *Hoard of Thunder 2: Philippine Short Stories in English* by UP Press. She has also written storybooks for children, *Si Lola Apura at si Lolo Un Momento*, published by Adarna House and *Ang Bisikleta ni Kyla*, a volunteer book project published by Philam Foundation.

Her latest work is a science fiction trilogy, the *Driftland* series, written for young adult readers.

The Waters
of Manila Bay
Are Never Silent

I.S.A. Crisostomo-Lopez

PENGUIN BOOKS

An imprint of Penguin Random House

PENGUIN BOOKS

USA | Canada | UK | Ireland | Australia
New Zealand | India | South Africa | China | Southeast Asia

Penguin Books is part of the Penguin Random House group of companies
whose addresses can be found at global.penguinrandomhouse.com

Published by Penguin Random House SEA Pvt. Ltd
9, Changi South Street 3, Level 08-01,
Singapore 486361

First published in Penguin Books by Penguin Random House SEA 2022
Copyright © I.S.A. Crisostomo-Lopez 2022

10 9 8 7 6 5 4 3 2 1

ISBN 9789815017991

Typeset in Garamond by MAP Systems, Bangalore, India

www.penguin.sg

This book is dedicated to all human rights victims who were unjustly tagged as drug users, drug pushers, and drug runners, including those who were summarily killed under the government's anti-drug campaign 'Oplan Tokhang', and those who were illegally detained, abused, tortured and killed during the Martial Law years in the Philippines (1972–86), including the *desaparecido*s or those who went missing and were presumed dead.

Contents

Introduction

Manila Bay lies on the south-western extremities of Luzon, a major island in the Philippine archipelago. It is a semi-enclosed estuary that is connected to the South China Sea. The bay has a surface area of approximately 1,800 sq. km and a coastline spanning 190 km. Its latitudinal and longitudinal coordinates are 14°16′N–15°0′N and 120°28′E and 121°15′E, respectively.

The bay serves as the port of Manila, the capital city of the Philippines. The easternmost part of the bay is divided into two harbours: North Harbour for inter-island ships and South Harbour for international shipping.

This almost-land-locked bay forms a natural harbour and provides excellent protected anchorage, owing to the mountains of Bataan Peninsula in the west and the Cordillera Central in the east.

The bay is intersected by seventeen river systems: Angat, Bocaue, Sta. Maria, Marilao, Meycauayan, Obando, Talisay, Guagua, and Pampanga rivers in Region 3; Meycauayan-Valenzuela, Pasig, Parañaque and Malabon-Navotas-Tullahan-Tinajeros rivers in the National Capital Region; and Imus, Ylang-ylang, Rio Grande and Cañas rivers in Region 4A.

River Pasig is one of the major rivers that connects Manila Bay to Laguna de Bay, the largest freshwater lake in Southeast Asia.

Coastal cities surrounding the bay include Manila, Pasay, Parañaque, Las Piñas, and Navotas as well as the coastal provinces of Bataan, Pampanga, Bulacan and Cavite, all of which accounts for around 30 per cent of the country's population.

As the capital city's port, Manila Bay is the gateway to the country's seat of political power. In 1571, the Spanish fleet sent by Miguel Lopez de Legaspi conquered the early Muslim kingdoms of Rajas Lakadula, Matanda and Sulayman in the Battle of Tondo. Consequently, Spain declared Las Islas Filipinas as a Spanish colony—named after the Spanish monarch Philip II—unifying 7,641[1] islands of the archipelago under one territorial domain.

As the only Spanish colony in Asia, the Philippines was recognized as an important outpost and centre of trade between 1565 and 1815. It formed the western terminus of the Manila-Acapulco route of the Galleon Trade. Manila became the capital of the entire Spanish East Indies.

Despite the occasional uprisings, which were quickly subdued, Spanish colonizers could exercise their authority without much trouble because the locals were mostly subservient, hospitable, industrious and peace-loving.

So, for more than 300 years, the indigenous people endured the oppressive labour system imposed on them and resented the discriminatory treatment meted out by the colonizers, particularly the Spanish friars. Subsequently, the mounting social oppression; public executions of alleged insurgents; and patriotic writings of propagandists José Rizal, Graciano López Jaena and Marcelo Del Pilar fanned the flame for a national sentiment to fight for independence.

Throughout Filipino history, the bay stood witness to many battles and revolutions fought by the people in their struggle for freedom. Seven of the eight provinces that revolted against the Spanish colonizers are part of the Manila Bay area—Manila,

---

[1] Taken from the website of the National Mapping and Resource Information Authority: www.namria.gov.ph

Laguna, Cavite, Batangas, Bulacan, Pampanga, Tarlac and Nueva Ecija.

Revolutionaries carried out the fight for freedom under the Katipunan, a secret society led by Andrés Bonifacio. The revolution that began in 1896 was initially centred in the province of Cavite, but it quickly spread across the major islands.

In 1898, when revolutionaries were on the brink of winning the war with the declaration of independence and the establishment of the first Philippine Republic by Emilio Aguinaldo, Spain ceded the Philippines to the United States under the Treaty of Paris. A mock naval battle called the Battle of Manila Bay signalled the end of Spanish rule in the Philippines.

The Filipino struggle for independence continued with guerrilla warfare against American troops. It ended only after the Second World War when Filipinos fought alongside Americans against the Japanese. In 1946, an independent Filipino republic was declared under the Treaty of Manila that relinquished American sovereignty over the Philippines.

More than two decades later, in 1972, the nation experienced another form of subjugation when Martial Law was declared under the administration of President Ferdinand E. Marcos. With the suspension of civil law, including freedom of speech and assembly, the people were forced to silently suffer under the oppressive rule of an authoritarian government. The economy plunged into turmoil; the national treasury was plundered; press freedom was suppressed; and freedom fighters were abducted, tortured and killed.

In February 1986, the people finally found the courage to stand up against the dictator in a protest rally on Epifanio de Los Santos Avenue (EDSA), a main thoroughfare in the metropolis. Armed with flowers and rosaries, the peaceful protesters demanded an end to violence, abuse and electoral fraud. They wanted to give peace and freedom a chance. The military, who also shared the sentiments of the masses, joined the protest. This resulted in a miraculous bloodless revolution that overturned the Marcos dictatorship, known worldwide as the EDSA People Power Revolution. Thus ended a dark and tumultuous chapter in the history of the 'pearl of the Orient', and freedom and peace were restored again in this beautiful land.

As the port of Manila, the bay is also the hub of commercial and industrial activities such as commercial fishing, aquaculture, shipping and tourism. Manufacturing industries are also located near the bay in industrial parks, both in coastal and non-coastal areas. However, Manila Bay faces severe sustainability issues from industrial and household pollution, illegal fishing and overfishing, marine habitat destruction, siltation and sedimentation, overexploitation of natural resources, and uncontrolled development in the form of land reclamation and most recently in 2021, the creation of an artificial beach. As of today, there are ongoing efforts by various government agencies to clean up, rehabilitate, restore, maintain, and preserve the waters of Manila Bay.

With its incredible natural beauty, rich and colourful history, and pristine water reflecting a modern skyline, Manila Bay is most admired for its breath-taking sunsets in warm and breezy afternoons and its freedom-loving people who are just as warm.

To an outsider, Manila Bay offers respite from the noise and action of the city. But for Zechariah 'Zeke' Dipasupil, who grew up on the busy streets of Manila, the sound of the bay's tranquil waters not only calms and clears his mind and conscience but also invigorates him to act and rise against the sweeping tides of silence.

Chapter One

Peace Seeker

Sometimes when the noise gets too loud in your head and the pressure makes you restless, you seek a place where the only sound is the low thumping inside your chest and the passage of air in and out of your system. But, here in the city where the lights never dim and the streets are seldom empty, it is almost impossible to get out of the glare to find a peaceful spot.

—Zechariah 'Zeke' Dipasupil

What could be more peaceful or romantic than walking along a beach and watching the sun dip into the horizon, the sky a beautiful haze of yellow, orange and purple? It was like watching the end of a play with the lights dimming slowly, the curtains being drawn, and the stage a glistening body of water—rolling and flowing. It seemed like it was applauding the end of the day with soft clapping sounds as the sun bid the day goodbye.

'Don't you just love the sound of the waves?' Zeke's mother said as she parked herself on the shore with her son and a picnic basket in tow.

Her eyes closed; she held her head high to get a better feel of the salty breeze blowing against her face. She smiled as a feeling of calm exhilaration washed over her entire being.

'Yes, Mama,' Zeke replied, like any other child agreeing with their mother.

As a young boy, Zeke loved to stroll on the beach with his mother. He liked its raw, salty, pungent smell that somehow cleared the passage to his lungs and helped him breathe more easily. Zeke liked the feeling of his wet feet. Occasionally, his mother would even let him take a dip in the shallow waters near the beach, a pastime he especially loved. There was always something interesting to see at the beach.

Zeke wouldn't miss the white seabirds for anything. With his camera, he would snap at the low-flying birds with their matchstick legs almost touching the water. The birds made him feel dreamy if not wistful; their presence made him feel like something magical was about to happen. But then his thoughts would be disrupted by a soft meow. How could he forget the cats! There was always one looking straight at him, begging for scraps. In fact, a sizeable number of them would be roaming among the open-air cafes like free spirits, getting food from the pet-friendly and 'shoo-shoo's from the zoophobic. But the cats weren't afraid of Zeke. They would rub their furry bodies against his leg, seemingly asking for a fraction of his attention. They would purr softly and present themselves as adorable. But for someone like him hoping for a miracle in dreamland, the cats—so associated with everyday city life—would zap him back to reality rather quickly and unwillingly.

Before their trip back home, Zeke's mother would buy him some ice cream, chocolates, or cotton candy from one of the many stores that dotted the bay walk. These would always sweeten his tongue and memory like a memento of a good trip.

Growing up in Tondo, one of the old districts of Manila, Zeke never got accustomed to the noise surrounding him—the zooming sound of jeepneys plying the streets, the shrieks of neighbourhood children playing, and the rattling sound of the light rail transit. Even the hawkers never seemed to sleep, their echoing cries reverberating through the bay area—pandesal at the break of dawn, taho at mid-morning, and balut at sunset.

Though these things robbed him of peace and quiet, Zeke accepted them as a part of the daily rituals of his childhood, a source of comfort and joy. Zeke couldn't imagine breakfast without pandesal, half-dipped in coffee or with fried eggs on the side.

Like most snack-loving children, Zeke too got a kick from hearing the taho vendor passing by. He would look forward to savouring the soft and sweet goodness of taho rolling in his mouth, or tucking into a typical supper with balut. He was especially proud of eating it without cringing and would never forget to top it off with a dash of salt and spicy vinegar—the spicier, the better.

Despite all the commotion, the sea was also a source of comfort for Zeke. It offered him solace, and he enjoyed every minute he spent near it. Like his mother always said, a body of water brought peace—its sound and smell, and especially the breeze that blew over it; all of these things created a sense of calm that healed tired nerves and rejuvenated the spirit.

* * *

Zeke never outgrew his fondness for a quiet place. With mounting pressure at work as a news editor and managing director of the city's largest daily newspaper, Zeke sought refuge in quiet places whenever he got the chance.

On a lucky day, he found such a place right in the heart of the city. Situated several stories high above the ground and adorned with plants and vines hanging on trellises, this was the rooftop of the newly constructed skyscraper—the Everglade Tower. It provided the perfect hideaway for anyone searching for some peace and quiet in the middle of a concrete jungle.

Zeke was attending a press conference at the tower and during the break, he enquired about where the smoking lounge might be. The building attendant, a lethargic man with tired-looking eyes, looked at him rather impassively. But upon recognizing him as a prominent journalist, stood up straight, cleared his throat and tried to respond respectfully without sounding offensive, 'Sir, other building tenants were clamouring to have one, but the building owner decided against it—for environmental reasons. She wanted the new building to be clean.'

'Oh! That's a shame,' Zeke quipped, while taking a deep breath in an effort to contain the growing frustration inside.

The media conference had started early. It was organized by the Chief of Staff of Senator Lustro to announce the good senator's bid to run for vice-president in the coming elections.

From an outsider's point of view, Zeke was there as an esteemed member of the press. Nobody knew that he was an unofficial member of the senator's payroll, a ghostwriter for the senator's speeches and his weekly newspaper column.

Personally, Zeke never liked the senator. The man had always been crafty and manipulative. Zeke first met him while covering a golf tournament that was organized to raise funds for children living in conflict-ridden areas in Mindanao.

Zeke hated the permanent wry smile on the senator's face— the same smile he had on when he coerced Zeke to draft an essay of sorts for him about the tournament and the importance of sharing one's resources with those who need it most.

'What's one essay?' he remembered the senator saying. 'It's all for a good cause. Think about the children.'

After that essay came another, and another, and before long, the senator had been invited to share his thoughts and ideas on a weekly column called 'A Good Cause'. And, with that, Zeke's fate as a de facto member of the senator's communication team was sealed.

As with all his writing assignments, Zeke barely had any sleep the night before. The senator sent several sounds of revisions to his speech, so much so that Zeke had lost count.

The brewed coffee at the snack table was not helpful at all. He was still sleepy and couldn't stifle a yawn. He needed a quiet place at least for these thirty minutes. Plus, his hands were quivering for a cigarette. He wanted a smoking lounge. No—he needed one badly. Otherwise he might become unreasonably irritable.

Before he turned to leave, the building attendant noticed his disappointment. He took him aside and whispered, 'Sir, if you want, I can lend you the key to the rooftop. It's the only place without a smoke detector.'

Zeke didn't see that coming. He felt embarrassed. He felt like a little boy throwing a mental tantrum who was suddenly pacified with a lollipop.

So he took the key as discreetly as possible but not without returning the favour. He handed a folded bill when he felt no one was looking.

Since that encounter, the rooftop of the Everglade Tower had become a secret hideaway for Zeke whenever he wanted to be by himself. He would look for Rey, the building attendant. In exchange for the lolly, he would give Rey something. Sometimes when he had no cash on hand, he would give Rey a box of red-labelled cigarettes or some really nice mint candies, the kind that comes in small tin boxes.

But given the increasing pressure of his workload lately, which made him frequent the rooftop and cause the receptionist to eye him suspiciously, Zeke had to devise some sort of dialogue.

'May I speak with Rey? Got a little problem only he can fix,' Zeke would tell the building receptionist with a little look of anxiety, just for effect.

He would feel curious eyes staring or meddlesome ears wanting to know more about what his problem might be. And when Rey finally came to meet him, he'd blurt out, 'This is a bit embarrassing! My ... uh ... mother-in-law's toilet is acting up again.'

The moment he said this, all curious eyes and ears would return to their former preoccupations, oblivious and unconcerned.

For Zeke, smoking was more of a ritual, not a whim. Unlike the others, he smoked only when he needed to think something over. So he referred to the nicotine-infused rolled-up tobacco leaves stick as his 'thinking stick' and the rooftop as the perfect 'thinking spot'.

Whenever he lit a 'thinking stick', he sent a signal to his brain to drop everything and focus all neurons towards one thing—that one thing that needed to be dissected, scrutinized, and thoroughly examined a million times over before a decision could be made.

Among his friends, only his best friend Kit didn't understand the concept of the 'thinking stick'. She was the level-headed type, not one who is easily swayed.

One time he tried to reason with her, justifying why he smoked by himself on the roof of a building. 'Smoking eases the nerves and relaxes the muscles, which helps the brain concentrate better. The elevation from the ground is a factor too. The higher you go up, the better your chances of thinking straight. I'm not sure if it is the thinning air or the weaker pull of gravity. But whatever it is, there is something special about high places that clears the mind and fortifies the spirit. Even Jesus took to the mountains to get away from the crowd!'

When Kit gave him a I-am-not-buying-that-crap look, Zeke tried another route. He tried to sound a bit philosophical if not altruistic. 'Smoking also taught me to take in only a puff, just the amount you need and breathe out as much as your lungs will allow. When you give more than what you take, fate will be kinder to you.'

He couldn't forget the way Kit rolled her eyes before giving him the sweetest smile to show him that she was doing him a great favour by keeping the friendship alive despite him being a pain in the ass.

With Kit's firm stand against smoking, Zeke tried not to smoke around her. Still, he kept a few sticks in his office drawer to help him whenever he felt that certain predicaments needed a good think before a solution could be found for them. And if nothing else, at least the stick made the situation bearable.

Listening to Senator Lustro speak at the media conference was a form of torture, which Zeke felt could be relieved by a few puffs. It was unbearable. The man's craggy face with his skin furrowed like a bulldog wasn't a pretty sight. But despite this, the senator, who was running for the second-highest position in the land, was a sweet talker. He had memorized his speech so well that Zeke could have sworn that the words were actually his, a sincere outpouring from his heart and not penned by someone else. But knowing the senator's devious character and the many shady transactions associated with him, the disparity was undeniable. His speech sounded like a farce.

Really? Zeke couldn't help but raise his eyebrows in disbelief.

For several weeks now, since he was made privy to the senator's plan to run for vice-president, he wanted out. The campaign trail would require a great deal of planning and execution, not to mention a large number of speeches, slogans, scripts and other material that would need to be penned. On the upside, he need not come along but knowing the senator, his phones and inboxes would definitely be burning and sleep would be an extravagance he couldn't afford.

Quitting was not an easy choice, especially these days. Zeke needed to rethink this matter a million times over because if he quit, he would lose the monthly retainer fee, which was a hefty sum. A large chunk of it funded school fees, books, and lunch money of more than a hundred indigent students in Mindanao who couldn't afford them. In short, the amount was for a good cause.

A small chunk, of course, went to his thinking stick! His thrifty ego wouldn't allow him to burn his own money. So, he got a benefactor instead.

Am I quitting to save myself the trouble, annoyance, and discomfort of working for this man? Will quitting do good to those kids who were trying to get some education?

He let out a sigh. For now, he just had to find the strength and fortitude to put up with this charade.

Chapter Two

Prayers and Deadlines

God, are you there? 'Cause I really need to know why you let these things happen to me.

—Zechariah 'Zeke' Dipasupil

Zeke considered every roadblock, every challenge, as a test of his faith. As a Catholic, he believed in a more powerful being who watched over him from heaven and had a great plan for his life.

The idea of God had always baffled Zeke as a child. His young mind marvelled at how someone so knowledgeable, omnipresent, and super powerful could have created every good thing in the world just by the words that sprang forth from his mouth.

What he liked the most was when God stopped the pervading darkness by commanding light. Thus, light came to be associated with God, like peace in the middle of chaos and truth in the face of deceit or ignorance.

Believing in the goodness of God, Zeke had hoped that God would also give him the answers to the questions troubling him: Who is my father? What happened to him? Is he dead? Why doesn't my mother want to talk about him? Why does she have chest pains? Why is she always crying? Why do her eyes look sad even when she's smiling? Why do I lose my voice whenever I feel anxious? What happens to my tongue? Does it get tied up at the back of my throat? Are people really whispering behind my back that I'm a freak? Do I have a grandfather and a grandmother like other kids? Where are they? Are they dead? Why are we alone?

In his quest to find answers to his questions, he was drawn to seek God in prayer during his early years in school.

As a third-grader who seldom spoke in class, he would finish his sandwich and empty his juice box in a hurried manner during recess. He would then whip up an excuse for his friends so he could leave the cafeteria and spend the remaining time in the school chapel situated on a hill, giving it the moniker Chapel Hill. Hurriedly, he would traverse the long empty corridors, follow the path to the garden, and hop from one concrete slab to another leading to the sanctuary of prayer.

He liked the way the chapel was built on an elevated slope on the east side of the school. He was fond of climbing up the steps leading to the iron gates of the entrance. A pond with a few koi fish and a garden that sat next to it added to the tranquillity of the sacred place.

Zeke would sit in silence on the pew made of polished mahogany wood and gaze upon the image of Christ with red-and-white rays radiating from his heart. It was an image of Jesus as the Divine Mercy, a devotion that stemmed from apparitions received by a mystic nun from Poland.

He would stay in Chapel Hill for several minutes, waiting for the bell to ring.

During those precious minutes of waiting and looking at the venerated image, Zeke had hoped to hear God's voice revealing the answers to his questions to help him understand why things happened to him as they did. But he was only met with silence.

Zeke's young mind believed that God was really busy elsewhere, answering other people's questions. This made him consider a hundred other possibilities—maybe other people had more urgent questions than him or perhaps they were more serious and complex, requiring a lot of time and effort from God.

Maybe after that, God got tired and needed to rest and resume his work the next day. Maybe the prayers of people from different parts of the world were so many that the angels were overwhelmed and exhausted themselves.

Maybe his prayer got lost under a mountain of prayers.

Maybe he should just be patient and wait his turn.

So, he spent more time at Chapel Hill and waited some more.

As weeks turned into months, Zeke realized he didn't mind the silence at all. He wasn't impatient or angry at God. If fact, he would return to Chapel Hill again after his last class before taking the ride home. He had learnt to enjoy the silence because it put his mind at ease.

Then one day, he heard it: 'Do you trust me?'

Zeke was in the chapel staring down at his shoes when he thought he heard a voice. It was faint yet distinct. It was a male voice, and it sounded gentle and peaceful. He felt like a guitar with his soul as the guitar strings being strummed ever so gently that a rippling deep inside him shook his whole being.

The odd sensation prompted his heart to beat faster than usual and his lungs to work double time to take in more oxygen. It was not like the fear that came from watching horror movies but a pleasant kind of fear tinged with excitement and wonder.

Straining his ears to listen more closely, Zeke heard the voice again: 'Do you trust me?'

Realizing the voice was real and not one that he had imagined, he ran out of the chapel, shocked and confused. The strange experience scared him—his heart was racing; he was almost out of breath. His shaky knees were unable to cope with the command from his brain to run faster, and he tripped on one of the concrete slabs. But he quickly got up and ran all the way back to his classroom.

He sat in class breaking in a cold sweat and looked straight at his teachers like a statue. He had a spooked-out look on his face that kept his classmates guessing the whole day.

'What's gotten into him?'

'The freak looks sick.'

'Maybe he should go home.'

'I saw him running from Chapel Hill. Maybe he saw something.'

'What do you think he saw?'

'Maybe an apparition?'

Zeke knew his classmates were whispering behind his back and talking about him, asking why he was acting so strangely. But even if he were to tell them, they wouldn't believe him anyway. Zeke knew better than to bother about them.

But what if he told Kit, his closest friend and ally? Maybe she would believe him. She sat next to him in class and had always been a good friend and confidante. Sometimes, she would even go out of her way to protect him from bullies.

On second thought, maybe she won't. Kit was the most level-headed person he had ever met. She wasn't the type who patronized hearsay. She could wring out the truth from anyone and tone down the distractive murmurs of the naysayers. Maybe she would think of the incident as too improbable and tell him that he was imagining things to the point of hearing them aloud.

And so, Zeke decided to keep everything to himself. Besides, what was the use? Even he couldn't make sense of what had transpired that morning following the second Sunday of Easter at Chapel Hill. How could others believe when he himself wasn't sure about what he heard?

Did God just talk to me? What did he mean by that?

* * *

Years passed and Zeke never heard the voice again. Or, maybe the voice spoke again but was drowned by the noise around him. Or, maybe he wasn't listening hard enough. The cacophony of everyday life was a lot to bear, making things go by unnoticed, whether mundane or otherwise.

Being a news editor and managing director of a local daily wasn't exactly a dream job for an ex-seminarian. Juggling the two roles didn't come easy either. While he had aspired to become a journalist when he was young, he never expected that he would land two jobs at the same time. The opportunity came like a gust of wind, surprising and totally unexpected. There was no inkling or calling to take up the mission unlike the time when he entered the seminary.

Zeke had always been drawn to the church because of its serenity as a house of prayer. Spending a few quiet minutes at Chapel Hill back in the day always made him feel better. So it wasn't a surprise when he told his mother that he wanted to become an altar boy during his teenage years.

He had always liked long prayer vigils as much as the solemn processions during Lent and other holy occasions. But what he enjoyed most was attending the holy mass and carrying a small bell made of brass that he would ring during the consecration ceremony. For him, the sound of the bell had a sacred quality that somewhat appeased God's wrath. And as the bell ringer, he felt as if he was, in a way, interceding for others.

After high school, Zeke had felt a strong calling to enter the seminary. There was something in theology and philosophy that appealed to him, which eventually captivated and hooked him like a noose around a mule's neck.

While reading the Book of Proverbs, he was struck by the passage, 'For the Lord gives wisdom; from His mouth comes knowledge and understanding.' For Zeke, gaining wisdom was the answer to the mysteries he couldn't explain, including the many unanswered questions in his life.

But as they say, time is the greatest teller of the truth. It probes the heart, tests the mind, and explores how far the spirit is willing to go.

The silence within the seminary walls was comforting at first. Everything was peaceful, calm and serene. At the break of dawn, he would wake up to the sound of nothing. He would kneel by his bedside and say a quiet prayer before folding his blanket in place. He was assigned to the kitchen to help in the preparation of meals but was forbidden to go out of the seminary.

In the kitchen, he would strain his ears to hear the sound of slicing, chopping, boiling and frying. Yet he failed to hear any as if the pots, pans and utensils were also trained for the silence of cloistered life.

At the dining table, everyone would gather together to say grace in a whisper, then swiftly empty their plates and glasses like it was a sin to chew and enjoy the food.

He had told his superior that he found everything too disturbingly quiet. The absence of sound gave an impression of cessation of life. He felt numb and everything turned grey and drab until he could no longer stand the deafening silence. He longed to hear the noise of the living—chatter, shrieks and laughter, stomping and shuffling of moving feet, and beeps and booms of cars and trucks. He longed to be connected again to the world outside.

After he left the seminary, he got a call from a high school friend seeking his help on a news article. His friend needed fresh eyes to look over it for any errors.

His human side could have politely declined the request since he felt he didn't have the expertise needed for the job. But his humanitarian side won over; he wanted to help those seeking help.

So, he read the draft with sharp eager eyes. Besides, reading was like second nature to him. He liked to read as a child. Books had kept him entertained for hours without the need to start a conversation.

Then, as if his efforts were rewarded by the universe, he was offered another proofreading job, and another, until his friend asked him if he wanted to apply for the position of field reporter.

Zeke felt as if the universe had already made prior arrangements for him to be at that exact spot at that exact moment and created an opening for him to walk right in. After several transfers, fill-ins, and promotions, Zechariah 'Zeke' Dipasupil became news editor and managing director of *The Manila Daily Star*, the largest daily newspaper in the city.

Becoming a journalist and editor was a fulfilment of his childhood dreams. Zeke felt that there was always something going on, something to tell, something to learn from. And it was every journalist's credo to uphold the truth and tell the world about it.

For more than a decade, he had dealt fairly but firmly with reporters, correspondents, proofreaders and desk editors every day, from bossy colleagues to shirkers. There were those who insisted their stories were privileged information, harder to find and should be given top priority. There were those who would submit their stories beyond the 5 p.m. deadline with a plea for mercy and reconsideration since, they claimed, there were unforeseen factors in the field that prevented them from beating the deadline.

'Connection was really bad. I had to find a good spot before I was able to send the email.'

'You can't imagine how hard it is to get an appointment with the mayor, the congressman, or the senator.'

'The assistants of these big-time people think they are big time themselves. They weren't really the accommodating type.'

'I lost my phone when I was eating at this small dining place. You also know what it feels like to lose your phone, right? It's like losing half of your life!'

'I know you got a heart inside your chest. It wouldn't hurt to reconsider every once in a long while.'

He would tell them squarely. 'The line is dead. It wouldn't be fair to those who kept a close watch on their clocks. The door is closed. Those who are left outside will gnash their teeth.'

They hated him for replying with words from the Bible because there was no way to go against it or around it.

'On the bright side, your stories will be considered for the next issue. Feel free to send an update, if any, before the 5 p.m. deadline tomorrow.'

Thanks to his uncompromising attitude and dedication to his profession, Zeke had earned a reputation as a prominent and well-respected journalist and media practitioner.

During the worst of times—which were more frequent than the good ones—when Zeke had come close to quitting, he would think of the reason why he couldn't have possibly stayed in the seminary where he was trained to shut out the noise and distractions to gain wisdom and enlightenment. Then, he would feel a tad grateful because journalism had taught him to be more receptive, to make wide open all his senses and use his faculties for the greater good. From there, enlightenment and wisdom would flow, giving light to his situation.

Chapter Three

Puzzles in Our Lives

Ever felt lonely despite being in the company of people because you feel like something or someone is missing? Your heart longs to be with the person who loves you, listens to you, and understands you like no one else does. You want to spend that special moment with her—your mother—but alas, she's too far away. You couldn't ignore the fact that somehow the separation dims the vividness of the moment, like a black and white filter, muffles the sound and intensity, and breaks your spirit little by little.

—Eliseo 'Jun-Jun' Reyes, Jr

Ever since his mother Aling Benilda left the country to work as an Overseas Filipino Workers (OFW), the boy Jun-Jun (or Eliseo Junior) grew up with his father and two younger siblings. They lived in a cramped two-bedroom apartment that sat in a row of apartment units inside a compound. His father Mang Jun (or Eliseo Senior) worked as a part-time electrician in a construction company and earned a meagre wage, just enough to provide subsistence to the family.

Money was scarce especially when there was no job order for Mang Jun. So Aling Benilda had agreed to live with a relative in Singapore and work as an all-around helper—cooking, cleaning, and taking care of young children. It pained her to be separated from her family but knowing her sacrifice would enable them to have a better life gave her strength and purpose.

Aling Benilda would come home every two years in time to attend the traditional Misa de Gallo with the family in December. The family would wake up early to attend the dawn masses held before Christmas, then tuck in delightful snacks like *bibingka* or *puto bumbong* on their way home from the church.

A devotee of the Santo Niño, Aling Benilda would participate in the feast day celebration that took place on the third Sunday of January. She would join other devotees in a festive parade, singing and dancing in the street while holding an image of the Child Jesus.

She had developed a personal devotion to the Child Jesus many years back when she was pregnant with her son Jun-Jun. Aling Benilda had almost lost her son to a miscarriage since her pregnancy was marred by occasions of bleeding. Her doctor had advised her to take bedrest and gave her medicines for her condition. For a long time, she had been anxious and unable to sleep soundly.

During those long periods of solitude in her room, Aling Benilda read old *stampitas* that had gathered dust inside a side table cabinet. The stampitas belonged to her late mother and were small enough to fit inside her apron pocket. They contained a short novena prayer to the Santo Niño for protection and guidance, especially for young children.

After reciting the prayer every morning upon rising and at night before going to bed, she felt comforted and was able to sleep well. The smiling image of the Child Jesus on the stampita somewhat eased her worries. At the end of the nine-day novena, she consecrated her unborn baby to the Child Jesus to protect him from harm.

When Jun-Jun was born, she was surprised to see how her son closely resembled the image of the Santo Niño whom she adored. The baby had brown curly hair, bright eyes like marbles, and big, round cheeks that made her want to kiss and cuddle him as long as she could.

But, unfortunately, she had to deal with the reality of her life, which was that she couldn't stay home to care for her children. She had to make the difficult decision to work abroad and earn a stable income to sustain her family.

Working as a housekeeper, Aling Benilda was tasked to buy food from the market, cook the family meals, ready the children for school, walk the family dog, take the laundry to the cleaners, and keep the owner's living quarters spic and span. It was located on the seventh floor of a mid-rise condominium building.

At night, after everyone had gone to sleep, Aling Benilda would look out the window and stare at the night sky, wondering how long she could endure the frequent pang of loneliness, the discrimination at the market, the too-heavy laundry bags, the allergies caused by the owner's pet, and her shrewd employers who oftentimes failed to pay her salary on time.

When at last she could come home, all her worries and anxieties would be rendered as things of the past, which could no longer affect her. She would arrive at the airport tired but beaming with delight, with three large *balikbayan* boxes in tow filled with chocolates, candies, body lotion and soap (to give away to relatives and neighbours), toys, cookies, clothes, shoes, canned goods, jackets, towels, blankets, among others, that brought joy and delight to her family—very much like Santa Claus and his big red sack full of goodies.

Her three children would hold a secret contest among themselves. The first to spot their mother from the crowd of people in the arrival area would win. The fastest runner to reach her would be the second winner. The two winners would get the privilege of opening the balikbayan boxes first and picking the things they liked. The loser would get what was left.

Jun-Jun, being the eldest would always spot their mother first. Whether she wore a hat, a scarf or shaded glasses or if she got a new hairstyle. Call it a son's instinct; he would always recognize her in the middle of a crowd. He knew her gait, the way her arm swung and her hips swayed as she walked. She had a distinct limp on her right leg, which was caused by a work-related accident a few years back. Her employers took pity and paid for her hospital bills, including her therapy.

Jun-Jun, who was kind-hearted and indulgent towards his siblings, would prop his younger brother, Angelo, up on a chair and let him take the credit.

'Hey, I saw Mama first!' Angelo would call out.

Almost instantaneously, Jun-Jun and his sister, Princess, would jump and race towards the direction that Angelo had pointed. For Jun-Jun, it was all a show. He didn't really mean to race with his sister. He just wanted to pump up the excitement for their mother's homecoming.

Princess ran the fastest among the three siblings. She was two years younger than Jun-Jun and liked rough play, the kind that involved dodging, running, tumbling and jumping. And as she always outran her playmates, she would reach their mother first, falling into her outstretched arms. She loved to get a whiff of her nearness. It was the scent of a distant land, the scent of travel, the scent of adventure.

With Angelo and Princess winning the contest, Jun-Jun would settle for what the two didn't pick from the box. It didn't really matter to him. He was happy to see his siblings dipping their hands excitedly inside the box to pull out surprises. Above all, he felt complete because his mother was home. He was grateful and looked forward to it, even if such completeness happened only every other year.

* * *

Since Aling Benilda was not with them most of the time, video calls were their only line of communication. Despite the distance, she always made sure she was involved, especially in the milestones in their lives—and Jun-Jun's acceptance to the Science High School was one of them.

Since his early years in school, Jun-Jun had shown an aptitude for science. He was amazed by the structure of atoms and molecules. He knew the periodic table by heart, and how the elements combined and produced different chemical reactions. He would join and win science quiz contests and competitions as a representative of his school. Come high school, he was able to pass the entrance examination to the city's Science High School. As a scholar, he was entitled to free tuition fees plus a monthly stipend.

His family was delighted with the good news but no one was prouder or more delighted than his mother.

Aling Benilda was in the park when she got wind of the good news. She was walking Cookie, her owner's black-and-brown Shih Tzu. She was resting on a bench and casually browsing the internet when she saw Jun-Jun's social media post. She almost shrieked with joy but was able to contain her excitement. With her quivering hands, she dialled Jun-Jun's number for a video call.

'Hello Anak, I saw your post. I'm so proud of you! But ... I wish you could have told me before posting it,' she said, unable to hide her disappointment.

'I'm sorry, Mama. Please don't be upset,' Jun-Jun begged. 'I had meant to call you last night but with a lot of things going on, I guess I forgot and fell asleep.'

Aling Benilda let out a sigh and paused to wipe the tears that had welled up in her eyes. She felt left out and wanted to sulk but she couldn't go on feeling that way for her son.

'It's okay Anak. I'm always here to support you,' she replied trying to keep her voice from trembling. She wouldn't want Jun-Jun to know that she had been an emotional wreck.

The next day, Aling Benilda sent money so the family could celebrate this milestone. And more importantly, for Jun-Jun to invite his friends and classmates to celebrate with him.

As early as four o'clock in the afternoon, upbeat dance music could be heard booming from a videoke machine that the family had rented for the party. Princess, Jun-Jun's younger sister, made use of her creative flair and transformed the vacant area inside the compound into a loud and festive party filled with silver and gold balloons, decorative buntings, and a large glittering banner that read: Congratulations, Kuya Jun-Jun!

The buffet table was filled with an assortment of food: *pancit sa bilao*, *lechong kawali*, *lumpiang shanghai*, chopsuey, pork barbecue, *leche flan* and *pichi-pichi* with fresh grated coconut on top.

They also ordered spaghetti, fried chicken and pizza from a popular fast-food chain.

A towering three-tiered cake stood at the centre of the dessert table because sweet tooth or not, a meal is never complete without finishing it with something sweet.

There were also several bottles of soda from Aling Caridad's sari-sari store down the street. Two cases of beer were also bought from the same store later that night by Mang Jun who invited his friends over.

'There's so much food, Papa. I only invited five of my closest friends in class plus our neighbours in the compound,' said Jun-Jun feeling rather overwhelmed. He was never really comfortable at parties, much less hosting one.

On the contrary, it was Mang Jun who appeared to be having a grand time. 'Don't worry, Anak. Since there's so much food, I invited my friends over from the construction. The *barangay* captain is also coming. We never really had a real party like this,' he said, feeling rather proud. Not only was he proud of his son's achievement, he was also delighted at being able to invite his friends and host such a party.

During the video call, Aling Benilda couldn't muffle her excitement.

'Congratulations again, Anak!' the older woman exclaimed in a high-pitched voice.

'Thank you, Mama,' said Jun-Jun, forcing a weak smile for his mother on camera.

'How was the party? Did you have a good time?' she asked, eager for more details.

'Uh ... yes, there's so much food ... My friends came and we took turns singing in the karaoke ... But I really wish you were here ... ' replied Jun-Jun, with a sound of longing in his voice.

'I'm sorry, Anak. I'll try to make it up to you. I promise,' she replied, wondering if being away from her children to earn better was still worth the sacrifice. She couldn't blame her son for feeling that way.

Aling Benilda had sensed the longing in his voice that he tried to mask with a smile. He wanted to be happy but couldn't. Must she always apologize for not being present? Hearing his words devoid of happiness felt like a sharp slap on her cheek, a dagger piercing through her heart.

As for Jun-Jun, seeing the guests dancing underneath the glittering decorations, some attempting to chit chat amid the deafening music and children running around the table overflowing with food and drinks, he felt lonelier than ever. Things were just not complete without his mother.

As the night wore on, the noise inside the compound began to tone down as guests took their leave. The older men stayed behind for another round of beer and laughs, taking their turns to sing Frank Sinatra's 'My Way', a classic Karaoke favourite.

Jun-Jun wished his mother were there to celebrate with the family. But thinking again, he understood that people made certain sacrifices for those they love. And in return for those sacrifices, he felt that he should at least be grateful and not resentful.

Hearing his father, Mang Jun, singing loudly with his drinking buddies on the karaoke, looking at Angelo fast asleep on the mattress, and Princess combing her hair in front of a large dresser cabinet mirror as she readied herself for sleep, Jun-Jun consoled himself that life was still good.

Chapter Four

Secrets That Destroy

Darkness has its way of inviting us in. When we choose to keep things in the dark, we inadvertently also step out of the light.

—Eliseo 'Jun' Reyes, Sr

With the dollar remittance sent by Aling Benilda at the end of each month, Mang Jun started drinking with his friends every Saturday night at the end of their work shift at the construction site. He had earned the moniker 'mayor' since he would offer to shoulder the expenses for beer and side dishes that would be bought from a sari-sari store and a nearby eatery.

'*Sagot mo yung beer, sagot namin yung kuwento.* (You pay for the beer, we'll take care of the stories.)' His friends would happily declare, since the stories and chitchats were always free.

During one of their drinking sessions, Mang Jun was introduced to a tall and burly man called Emong, who was newly hired by their foreman.

Mang Jun never liked the man's face—his eyes seemed to be discreetly observing, which were shaded by thick eyebrows like they were made to cover them for such purpose; his thick lips were purple from smoking, which reminded him of the unappetizing eggplants that his mother-in-law used to cook.

Emong appeared to be aloof and kept his thoughts to himself even when the whole gang was already drunk, noisy and riotous. For this reason, Mang Jun kept his distance, judging the newcomer's silence as unfriendly and anti-social.

On their third encounter, it was Emong who approached Mang Jun, asking for help about a certain electrical wiring plan of a building that they were constructing. Mang Jun gladly offered his assistance.

After helping him out, Emong appeared thankful and then made Mang Jun an offer. 'Do you want to earn extra cash? My way of returning the favour.'

'Don't mention it. It's nothing,' replied Mang Jun who suddenly felt awkward. He didn't like where the conversation was heading.

Emong sneered at him. 'Perhaps you didn't hear me right? I said I can help you earn extra, so you can surprise your wife when she comes home from abroad or buy something nice for the children.'

Mang Jun never liked Emong; he trusted him even less. But at that moment, he was afraid because Emong looked like he wouldn't take no for an answer.

'What do you mean earn extra? Are you referring me to a client?' Mang Jun asked, trying to hide his apprehension.

'You can say there is a client. But we don't need to meet them. We just need to do something for them, discreetly. Then afterwards, we get paid.'

Emong slipped a roll of money into his hands. The bills felt new and crisp; they smelt good, just enough to make him curious. But at the same time, Mang Jun felt all the more afraid, like something wasn't right.

'I'm sorry, I cannot accept it.' Mang Jun tried to return the money.

Emong smiled just enough to reveal a silver-capped tooth peeking at the corner of his eggplant-coloured lips. 'It will be easy money when you get the hang of it. That's the down payment. I'll give you the rest when the job is done.'

* * **

The task was simple. He would meet up with a man or woman at a specific time at a light rail train station and be handed over a bag. This would be during a short fifteen-minute window period when the dog handlers would change their shifts, after the K-9 unit had finished their inspection of the coaches. So, he would have to be at that exact spot at a specific time to receive the bag.

His task was to carry the bag, walking calmly and normally so as not to draw attention to himself. He needed to keep the bag safe and bring it to a specified place and leave it there. Somebody would receive the bag and take it away. Easy-peasy.

Whatever was inside the bag was irrelevant and none of his business.

After his first successful bag delivery, Mang Jun came home looking rather shaken. His right arm felt stiff from carrying the bag. It was quite a load. His palms were wet, making it harder to grip the bag handle and keep it from slipping from his hands.

But more than the physical exertion, the stress and anxiety were intense. It pervaded his entire being long after the task was done. He had never felt so nervous in his life, like his heart would jump out of his chest and run away, never to return.

When he got home, he was met at the door by his son Jun-Jun, who first noticed his tired and worried look and the way he trudged from the gate to their house.

'Is something wrong, Papa?' Jun-Jun asked.

'It's nothing. I'm just tired because we got a deadline to meet at a new site. I'm setting up the electrical wiring for a new condominium that the company is building,' he replied.

Mang Jun put down his backpack and helmet on the sofa. Unlike the other days, he could not sit down for a few minutes to rest. Though he was tired, the adrenaline in his blood made him restless. He couldn't keep still. His mind kept bugging him to see if the rolls of money inside his pocket were real.

So as soon as he dropped his backpack on the sofa, he went straight to the toilet. After locking the door, he took out three rolls of money from the pocket of his work suit. His hands were trembling. He removed the rubber bands and began to count the bills on top of the toilet tank, all crisp and smelling brand new. He had never laid his hands on this much money before.

After counting the last of the bills, he gasped, almost breathless in disbelief. The amount was triple his salary at the construction company. He couldn't believe the luck that had befallen him.

Then he thought about the nice things he could buy with the money. He marvelled at how quickly his brain processed the information. He could go to the mall with the kids and buy some new clothes for himself and the children. For a change, it would be nice to buy nice things without looking at the price tag.

In addition, he thought of getting some good things to eat, or better yet, going to a large members-only shopping centre— signing up for membership like rich people do—and filling their refrigerator with a month's supply of food. He need not make an account to his wife Benilda on how he spent the family budget.

He could buy himself a new watch or get the shoes he had always wanted to buy from the department store window.

He chided himself. *'Para ka namang bata na gustong bumili ng maraming kendi!'* (You're behaving like a child who wants to buy a lot of candy!)

Then, he thought about his late mother-in-law, who used to live with them. She used to nag him about saving something for the rainy days because she felt that he wasn't saving enough for the family. He smiled. He could still hear her raspy old voice in his head saying the old adage, *'Ubos-ubos biyaya, bukas ay wala.'* (If you spend everything now, you have nothing left for tomorrow.)

He never really liked his mother-in-law, and he knew the feeling was mutual. But, out of respect, he had her ashes contained in an urn that the family kept on their altar.

He found it funny and also strange how a dead person's admonition that he used to hate once upon a time seemed to make a lot of sense now. Perhaps in the past it didn't make sense because there wasn't enough money left to save from his meagre salary.

But times were changing. He could finally save money in a bank. Truth is, he never owned a savings account. Only his wife had a bank account which she used to send remittances home. Maybe with the money he had now, he could finally open an account under his own name.

Maybe money could also give him a louder voice in the family and put him on equal footing with his wife as a co-decision maker. Funny how money could change how things used to be.

He never liked the way his wife always dictated what was good for the family. He never liked the way she made him feel like a second-class citizen.

It was a good thing that he never liked confrontations. He never wanted a fight. He would rather keep his thoughts to himself than start a war. Thinking ahead, he felt that maybe now if he could save enough money, Benilda wouldn't need to work abroad. Maybe he could finally convince her to come home for good. And he would become the family's main provider, the decision maker, the King.

Money is really a life-changer.

But then an awful thought crossed his mind. What if the bank asks him for documents for the money under the Anti-Money Laundering law? Surely the amount would exceed his pay slip. What if they suspected that his money came from illegal sources? He wouldn't want to get caught. And, so, he quickly decided that no deposit would be made. No one needed to know about his secret business dealings. It would be safer that way.

In the days that followed, he busied himself with the task of finding a good hiding place to stash his not-so-hard-earned cash.

Chapter Five

Miracle from an Urn

Funny how we wanted to grow up fast to know more and understand more.
But the irony is, the older we get, the more complicated things become and we
pass on half-truths as truths when we should know better.

—Eliseo 'Jun' Reyes, Sr

A year after being admitted to the city's Science High School, Jun-Jun was now in Grade 8. He was able to sustain high marks in school while keeping his responsibilities at home. He was in charge of cooking the family meals and helping his siblings prepare for school every morning.

He would wake up early to cook breakfast, mostly made of rice, fried eggs and sardines. He would also pour hot water into cups containing 3-in-1 instant powdered coffee. Sometimes he would buy some *pan de sal* from the bicycle-riding vendor, who sounded his horn peddling bread in the neighbourhood as early as the crack of dawn. He would also prepare his siblings' lunchboxes with rice and sweet cured pork along with water bottles filled up with iced water that would sustain them for a good six or seven hours in school.

Princess, the second child, was in Grade 6. She was in charge of the family laundry, including folding and ironing clothes every Saturday. She would also make sure the clothes were properly folded, the wrinkles smoothened out with a hot iron, and hung neatly in their cabinet.

The youngest boy, Angelo, helped with the family chores by keeping the floor clean with a broom and mop. A bit of wax at the end made it shine. He would also water the plants and wash the dishes.

Every morning before they left the house for school, they would take their father's hand and touch it to their foreheads as a sign of respect. They also never failed to bid goodbye to their grandmother, whose ashes were kept in an urn on the altar. The urn was adorned with an intricate blue-and-gold pattern.

'We're off to school, Lola!' They would call out loudly to their dead grandmother as they passed by the urn on the altar. They would wait at the gate of their compound for the tricycle that took them to school.

Following this daily routine, Mang Jun waited for his children to leave the house for school.

When he was alone in the house, he took out a carefully wrapped package from a thrift and antique shop. It was an urn with the same design as the urn containing his mother-in-law's ashes, only slightly bigger. He had spotted it a few days back while window shopping. When he saw the urn, he decided that it was the perfect place to hide his money. No one would suspect it. And since it was presumed to contain a deceased person's ashes, no one would dare go near it or tamper with it.

But first, he must transfer the old urn with his mother-in-law's ashes to a columbarium. He had taken care of this too. With his money, he was able to rent a columbary vault and make an advance payment for three months.

Now with the children away in school, he could finally make the switch.

He felt his hands quiver as he took his mother-in-law's urn. It felt like the urn had suddenly turned cold to the touch.

'Mama,' he whispered. 'I know you don't like me as a son-in-law. But I still respect you. Fate has been good to us. I've finally found a better, more peaceful place for you to rest.'

Putting his in-law's urn on the table, he placed the new and bigger urn on the altar, took off its cover, unfurled several rolls of money and stuffed every last bit of it inside the empty urn. Then he replaced the cover on top.

He looked at his masterpiece and smiled. He felt like a genius.

Then another idea crossed his mind. Perhaps he could seal the cover with some sort of adhesive like epoxy or contact glue instead ... wouldn't it be safer that way?

But what if he ran out of cash? He would have a hard time opening the urn if he sealed it. But then again, what if Angelo or any of the children accidentally hit the urn while cleaning the house? Mang Jun certainly didn't want the money spilling out.

In the end, fretting over his dilemma, he decided to squeeze out a thin layer of contact glue around the cover to keep it in place. That way it would be easier for him to open it whenever he needed the cash.

* * *

It was Princess who first noticed the new urn. She thought it strange that her grandmother's urn appeared to be bigger if not different altogether. She called her kuya Jun-Jun to tell him about her observation.

'Kuya, there's something different about Lola's urn, don't you think?'

Jun-Jun looked at the urn closely and frowned when he saw that it had no cracks, looked cleaner and was slightly larger than he remembered. 'Yes ... I don't think it's the same.'

Angelo joined in the conversation and joked. 'Maybe Lola has grown a few centimetres while inside.'

'Gelo, it's not funny to make jokes about a dead person,' Princess gasped incredulously, admonishing her younger brother.

She turned to her older brother, eyebrows scrunched in worry, 'Kuya, do you think somebody stole Lola's ashes and replaced it with a new urn?'

'Let's ask Papa when he comes home,' ruled Jun-Jun.

But the children's observation fell on deaf ears as Mang Jun dismissed them outright, saying it was the same urn. He further argued saying that no one would take an interest in Lola's ashes and go to great lengths as to steal it or replace it with a replica.

'That's nonsense! Why would someone want to disturb the dead? It's the same urn for all I care.'

The youngsters were easy to subdue, and their voices were silenced. They shrugged and decided to accept their father's words as true.

With the issue quickly dismissed, the children went back to their morning routine of bidding goodbye to their grandmother's ashes as they passed by the altar before leaving the house—except a part of them remained doubtful, which translated to lesser enthusiasm.

'We're off to school, Lola. See you later,' they said rather impassively.

Mang Jun tried to hide his guilt by keeping a straight face, despite knowing that the urn contained money instead of his mother-in-law's ashes.

One night, as if fate had intervened to allow his secret to be revealed, Mang Jun was caught in the act by Jun-Jun. The older man had thought the children were fast asleep, so he went to the altar, grabbed the urn, pried open its cover, and reached in to grab some cash. He was just about to put the cover back when suddenly he heard a voice—

'Papa, what are you doing?'

It was Jun-Jun, who had woken up feeling thirsty. He was heading toward the kitchen for a drink of water when he saw his father holding the urn with its cover.

'Oh, how come you're still awake? I was just praying to your Lola the other night for a miracle because we don't have enough money to pay for your school projects. Your mother's remittance isn't due until the end of the month. And guess what happened?'

'What happened, Papa?' asked Jun-Jun, looking a bit sleepy.

'I dreamt that your Lola gave me some money. So I checked the urn. Now look!'

Mang Jun held up five crisp one thousand peso bills.

Jun-Jun, sleepy as he was, strained his eyes to focus on what his father was holding.

'Is that money? Real money?' Jun-Jun couldn't believe his eyes. It took a few seconds for him to realize what he was seeing then gave out a shriek of excitement.

'Wow, Papa! It's a miracle!'

'Yes, indeed it is! And look how new and crisp and fragrant the bills are, like they came from no less than heaven's ATM machine!' Mang Jun declared proudly.

Jun-Jun drew close and touched the money to see for himself.

'We're not dreaming, are we, Papa? The money looks real enough to me.'

Mang Jun was irked. 'Of course it is real! But let's not overdo it. We shall only pray to your Lola for money when we really need it.' Mang Jun proclaimed with an air of authority.

'Yes Papa,' Jun-Jun agreed happily. After drinking a glass of water, he went back to sleep feeling grateful for the blessing that befell them.

Unlike Jun-Jun, Mang Jun lay awake on his bed, thinking how long he could keep the story going. He thought about the number one telenovela series running on primetime for five years straight. The writers must have been wrecking their brains thinking of a thousand ways to complicate the plot and keep the viewers glued and guessing what would happen next.

He grimaced at the thought of doing the same. It was something he had never done before.

Money was really a life-changer.

Chapter Six

Who Protects the Young?

The old is made to protect the young, the same way the strong is made to help the weak. The time will come when the tide will change—the strong will stumble and become weak and the young will gain strength to help the old.
—Zechariah 'Zeke' Dipasupil

The article came with a disturbing title: 'Boy, dead at 14, tagged as drug runner'. The email clocked in at 5:03 p.m. It was three minutes beyond the deadline.

Zeke read the article title again, then looked at the clock for the second time. He closed his eyes in frustration and felt as if he was doused in ice-cold water.

'Unbelievable … ' he muttered to himself. He felt as if fate was playing tricks on him, putting his good judgement to the test as to how far he was willing to bend his rules, that is, if he was willing at all.

His assistant news editor, Roy, noticed the change in his demeanour.

'You okay, Boss?'

Zeke took a deep breath. 'An article just came in. The line is dead. But I think I need to take a good look at it.'

His conscience was screaming: *The LINE is DEAD. But a BOY is DEAD too.*

His sane, impersonal and unemotional self was taking a firm stand. *You are not going to break your rules. You are not going to give an exemption,* he kept reminding himself, but no matter how hard he tried to divert his attention, his mind kept thinking about the dead boy. The article was screaming in a soundless but disturbing manner.

At his desk, Zeke pulled the lowest drawer open of his pedestal cabinet and fumbled for a cigarette. There was an unfinished pack; it still had two sticks left. He took one, grabbed his jacket and headed for the door.

'I'll be right back,' he told Roy.

The Everglade Tower stood on the corner of 5th Avenue and 26th Street. Towering at 329 metres, and with the addition of a communication tower or antenna on its rooftop, it was recognized as the tallest building in the city—its imposing structure cast a shadow over the surrounding buildings in the area.

'I need to see Rey. Is he in?' Zeke asked the receptionist, his hand unconsciously and impatiently knocking on the wooden surface of the receptionist's desk. The receptionist gave him a wry look before dialling Rey's extension.

The trip to the rooftop took longer than expected. The lift made stops on several empty floors, and with each one, the flurry of thoughts in Zeke's mind pounded at him more. It was only when he stepped onto the rooftop and saw the familiar lush greenery that he felt his agitation slowly dissipate. There was something in this green oasis that seemed to calm his nerves no matter how frazzled, in the same way that the sea of his distant childhood did. He found a comfortable place to sit on and lit a stick.

With dusk setting in, the cloudless sky was now a beautiful haze of yellow, orange and purple.

The sight of the hanging vines swaying in the wind somewhat made him breathe easier, as if a weight had been lifted off his shoulders.

Soon, the wind began to blow. It wouldn't be long before it got dark. How he wished time would slow down and let him savour the colours of dusk before everything turned black.

'Beautiful,' he said to himself as he admired the sky's changing hues. But the purple haze carried a sombre quality that was depressing.

He took a puff and began throwing questions to the wind. *What happened to him? How could he be dead at fourteen? Isn't it too soon for someone so young? Where were his parents when he needed them? What about his friends? Why hadn't someone done something to help him? How could a boy suffer at the hands of those who swore to serve and protect?*

Zeke's heart sank at the irony.

Then there was another voice in his head, sceptic and unfeeling.

People die every day for a lot of reasons. Maybe it's his turn to die. Who are you to judge that it was too soon? Every man to his own fate. Only God knows when your time is up.

Zeke felt sorry for the dead boy. He felt sad for the boy's parents, who would have to bury a son—blood of their blood and flesh of their flesh, a source of joy and pride, an heir who could have continued the family bloodline in the coming generations.

He thought about the boy's siblings, cousins, classmates, friends. *Did he have a girlfriend? A best friend, perhaps? How did they take the news? For sure there would be tears in their eyes, and shock maybe. Definitely, it would take a long time for their broken hearts to mend, if at all.*

The article said the boy's mother worked abroad as a domestic helper. He also had a younger brother and a sister. With empathy gnawing at his heart, he felt crushed for the grief-stricken family.

Zeke thought about the boy again. The article said he was a scholar at the city's Science High School. He must have been a smart boy, maybe even diligent. To be admitted to a Science High School requires good grades, which must be maintained, otherwise one would get transferred to a regular public high school.

His fingers quivered with a sense of loss and contempt. There was a feeling of regret he couldn't explain.

The boy could have been a star student in his class. Who knows what he could have become in the future? He could have been an engineer, a scientist, the city mayor.

How could his life have ended at fourteen? A boy's life should be exuberant and exciting, an ongoing adventure of ups and downs, of discovery and rediscovery, of failures and learning. There were so many things ahead of him. But alas, he couldn't experience them anymore because his time was up, or someone robbed him of the chance to continue living.

Zeke's hand continued to shake as he tried to hold on to the cigarette, which had burnt up to the filter.

Who could have done such a ghastly thing? What could be the motive behind the killing? Was it an accident? Was he a fall guy? Was he caught in the crossfire?

The wind was blowing hard against his face. The plants hanging on the trellis offered little resistance. Sadly, the wind didn't bring any answers to his questions.

It was getting dark. As much as he wanted to stay, time was up for him too. He must go back to the office. He didn't want his sub-editor to be overwhelmed by the number of articles that needed to be edited.

He got up and headed back to the lift.

As the lift door opened, Zeke was surprised to see a young lady. Her hair was immaculately combed in a bun although some streaks of hair colour were still visible. Judging from her uniform and nameplate, she appeared to be working in the building's housekeeping department. Strangely, her uniform seemed too big for her small frame. Her make-up, too, seemed out of place. It failed to mask her age. She was too young to be working.

'Good evening, sir,' she greeted him meekly, appearing just as surprised to see someone from the rooftop.

'Your name is Hestia?' Zeke read the name pinned on her chest. 'It's a beautiful name—the goddess of the hearth.' He was hoping to start a conversation to address the awkwardness.

'It's not really mine,' the girl stammered in reply. 'I'm filling in for a friend who's sick. It's a temporary arrangement until she gets well.'

'Oh, I see.' Zeke admired the girl's honesty, her blunt openness to a stranger about the way things were.

Zeke thought about the girl's lipstick. The red shade just didn't match her. But it made her look more mature if not attractive.

He thought of how she would look better if she had dressed her age. Funny how the young wanted to look older and the old wanted to look young. It seemed like nobody wanted to reveal the truth about their age, like it was something that wasn't meant to be revealed at all.

He thought that there was something about the youth and their tendency to adhere to the truth—something that they seemed to lose as they grew older. When adulthood set in, their judgement would become clouded, prompting them to tell the truth in a variety of ways.

After a few stops, the lift touched the ground. As its doors slid open, the girl quickly stepped out and disappeared among the people milling around the lobby.

Zeke saw Rey waiting for him. He slipped some bills into Rey's hand along with the key.

As he walked back to his office building, the image of the girl's innocent eyes kept popping in his head, taunting him; her truthful lips curled in distaste, admonishing him.

Chapter Seven

When Fire Meets Fire

No two kings can sit on the same throne at the same time because two great minds pulling towards the opposite direction will tear a kingdom apart.

—Benjamin Zultan

Since timeliness is of the essence in the newspaper industry, Zeke felt all the more strongly about publishing the dead boy's story for the next day's issue. It wasn't just a police story. For him, the story deserved more attention. He was bothered when he read it, and he felt like it should bother more people. Regardless of what the other editors might think, including the editor-in-chief himself, Zeke felt it merited more visibility in the newspaper. In fact, no less than the front page. He could position the story on one of the pages' ears. Or just below the banner story. But its true fate lay in the hands of Benjamin Zultan, the editor-in-chief of *The Manila Daily Star.*

Everyone knew that Mr Zultan was a hard man. No one wanted to ride with him in the lift—out of respect, or more appropriately, out of fear. He sported a bushy unibrow that magnified his already grumpy demeanour.

One employee who was a new hire had made the mistake of taking the lift with Zultan. She was seen running out of the lift with tears in her eyes. The girl immediately left the building and sent her resignation the next day.

When the HR manager asked Zultan what happened in the lift, he said, 'I asked her a simple question: "Have you read the morning news today?" She replied, "Not yet, Sir." So I told her, "Anyone who doesn't give a damn about what's happening around them doesn't have any business in this company." Now if she can't deal with the truth from what I said, then she's better off working in another company.'

His loud booming voice could scare a rabbit out of its skin. A well-travelled polymath, he was proud and irascible so no one dared enter his office. All interactions were limited to calls a little over a minute or less.

One time, an editor walked into Zultan's office, wanting to negotiate for space on the front page since an advertiser had called in making a handsome offer.

'Are you here to make the front page better or are you here to make a mess out of it?' asked Zultan, who was clearly annoyed whenever somebody proposed changes to his turf.

'Look at it this way, Sir. It's the company's fiftieth founding anniversary. They want their company history in a very prominent place and are willing to pay the price.'

'They should have reserved a space if they consider it really important and not a last-minute whim. Tell them that.'

'But Sir, if you will reconsider ... ' begged the editor. 'We seldom get offers like this. We can double or even triple the price if we want to.'

Zultan sneered like he'd smelt something going on. 'I hate to tell you this but if you have already sold your soul to the devil, I'm not here to save you. Now get out! And don't you dare show your face here again.'

* * *

The editors met again in a final budget meeting to finalize the line-up of news stories scheduled for the next day's newspaper.

The meeting was meant to get the final approval of all the editors before the final copy went to print.

As the meeting progressed, the editors reviewed the updated story submissions along with the images sent in by the photographers. There were just two breaking stories that were easy to absorb in the space that was left after all advertisements were laid out. Even Zultan was in a good mood since the meeting was almost over. But maybe not. Someone was raising his hand.

'Yes, Mr Dipasupil?' Zultan eyed him rather sourly from behind his glasses: this wasn't the first time that Zeke had interfered with the final list of stories on the front page.

'Sir, I know we seldom accommodate new stories in the list … unless the story is breaking news of utmost importance. But I'd like to bring to your attention a news story that just came in … it's about a boy who died at the hands of anti-drug police operatives. He was in Grade 8 and a scholar at the city's Science High School. He was tagged by police operatives as a drug runner.'

'Oh, that's so sad and unfortunate,' said one editor, leaning forward as if wanting to know more.

'A dead drug runner? What about it?' asked another rather impassively, while sipping coffee.

'He's dead, and he's only fourteen. Here's a copy for your reference,' said Zeke, as he passed around copies of the article.

An editor frowned and pursed his lips while reading the article. 'We get police stories with dead people in them all the time. What makes this any different?'

'A young and helpless boy died at the hands of armed policemen. Can't you see that something is clearly wrong here?' Zeke replied, his voice louder than usual.

'I agree that this can be alarming because children are getting killed,' concurred one editor, 'but come to think of it, in war, too, children get caught in the crossfire. A dead child and an armed solder—a sad picture, but it happens. We mourn and we move on.'

'Perhaps we should move on. It's getting late,' suggested another who leaned back on his chair, looking tired.

'Oplan Tokhang is the government's war against illegal drugs. But it's also churning out dead people every single day. Now young people are dying. Am I the only one bothered by it?' Zeke exclaimed as he slammed his hands on the table in frustration. Controlling his temper was Zeke's greatest weakness. And whenever he lost it, he always had a hard time pulling the reins on his tongue.

Zultan was quietly observing the word war. He wasn't amused.

'Mr Dipasupil,' Zultan's voice boomed like a bomb. 'You know time is of the essence. We can't afford any drama in the newsroom. We can't see the point of this argument. If you feel sad about that boy dying, you can take a day off.'

'Sir, I'm not seeking anyone's sympathy here. Can't you see the boy's a helpless victim? Can't you see that the young and the helpless are bearing the brunt of this anti-drugs campaign?' Zeke reasoned out, almost shouting. The heat was rising up to his ears.

The tone of Zeke's voice irked Zultan. 'Are you shouting at me?'

'With all due respect, Sir. If you or anyone else will just listen, I don't need to raise my voice.'

'I don't *need* to listen to you! You're wasting our time on this stupid article!' Zultan growled, his face turning from a furrowed dog into a snarling monster.

'Let it go, Zeke,' whispered one of the editors. 'There's no point arguing.'

'I have every reason to believe that this story should be on the front page of every newspaper in this goddamned city!' Zeke exclaimed in a loud voice.

'What you are asking is beyond your jurisdiction. You are stepping way beyond the line, you son of a bitch!'

'If I have to, I will!'

The other editors were dumbfounded as they watched the altercation between Zeke and Zultan. No one in their right mind had ever dared to engage with Zultan in a shouting match. They were trying to figure out if, at that moment, Zeke had indeed lost his mind.

Zeke's hands were trembling. There were beads of tears at the corners of his eyes. He was fuming mad because no one was listening to what he was trying to say. He didn't mean to shout at Zultan. Now, the man looked even more hideous.

'I shall have none of this nonsense. You're fired! Now get out!' Zultan's voice boomed and cracked. His patience had clearly run out.

'Go ahead, fire me for all I care. But this story is going to be big, and you'll be sorry because you didn't listen hard enough to what I was trying to say.'

'Get out of my sight! I don't need you to tell me what to do! Go before I call security!'

'No need. I can find my way out,' replied Zeke as he took his folder and pen and walked out of the meeting room.

The other editors slowly stood up and left the room one after the other. They had just seen the most feared man in the office, Mr Zultan, get his face all red with anger. He looked all the more fearsome, and it wasn't a pretty sight to behold.

The budget meeting table was round like that of King Arthur's. It was meant to signify equality among those who gathered around it. Yet, during actual budget meetings, there was only one big and powerful voice that dominated over the others. Other voices were rendered insignificant and always overruled.

But this time, somebody had spoken up despite waves of opposition. He had held his ground against the big and powerful voice, wanting and insisting on being heard. It was an unprecedented act because Zultan considered himself a god who wielded his power over the fate of every article that went into the newspaper.

As editor-in-chief, he had the final say on whether an article gets published or not, which article gets a major cut, and which merits space on the much-coveted front page.

Now, the big man had gotten a verbal beating from Zeke, who also happened to be the youngest and the brightest among them.

The incident was explosive, yet the sparks that flew were quickly extinguished with a curt, 'You're fired!'

Nobody expected the meeting to end this way. The editors looked at one another before sheepishly tracing their steps back to their desks. They were sad to see a good man go, sacked for voicing out his opinion, by the man who sat on top of the food chain ready to devour anyone who got in his way.

Chapter Eight

Empathy and Sympathy

Having sympathy for someone is like being in a circle separate from the other person's circle. You don't know how the other is feeling. But empathy is different. The two circles are merged together so that you feel and understand what it is like to be in another's situation.

—Zechariah 'Zeke' Dipasupil

Zeke stormed out of the editor's final budget meeting. He walked in hurried steps towards the Everglade Tower, unmindful of the rushing crowd going against his direction as he crossed the busy pedestrian lane. He needed a quiet place to sort things out. And he needed his 'thinking stick', fast.

On the rooftop, he sat at his favourite spot and observed the towering structures that surrounded him. He wondered if the people in those buildings also occasionally find themselves in a tight spot. Then, his eyes fell on a piece of gum wrapper tossed around by the strong current blowing. At that instant, he felt small.

He felt a mix of emotions—anger, frustration, and regret. He was mad at himself for saying the things that made Mr Zultan angry. He was frustrated that he had failed to justify in a calm and proper manner why the article on the dead boy should have been on tomorrow's front page. He regretted how things turned out at the meeting, which may, indeed, be his last as news editor and managing director of *The Manila Daily Star*—it had been his home and family for more than a decade—all because he let his emotions get the better of him.

Thinking again about the article, he couldn't help but feel emotional. Like the boy whose voice was silenced, he felt as if everyone in the meeting wanted him to shut up too.

Being young, the dead boy could have been easily looked down on and his rights trampled upon. Was he really a drug runner? Or was he a victim of his circumstances?

The police involved in the shooting could have been easily judged as preying on the weak and defenceless. Did they really shoot the boy in an attempt to stop him from eluding arrest? Or were they abusive and remiss in their duty to uphold the law and protect the innocent? If that was the case, then the act could only be described as ruthless and unforgivable. He would not be surprised if it was, what with everything that he had been hearing in the news. What if the boy had no one else to turn to? What if no one actually heard his plea?

He knew how that felt like—wanting to talk but unable to get the message across. He knew the pain, the frustration of opening one's mouth but having no sound comes out of it. Had the boy been in a similar situation? Had his voice been ignored and disregarded by his tormentors too?

All this thinking reminded Zeke why this entire incident affected him so much. He empathized with the dead boy because he too had lost his voice when he was young.

* * *

Zeke was a fourth grader sitting in the cardiologist's clinic with his mother. He would have liked to stay home and play with his toy cars and fire trucks but his mother's intermittent chest pains bothered him as it has been giving her sleepless nights.

What if she die? So, he tagged along to her scheduled check-up. He wanted to hear what the doctor had to say about her heart and the trouble with it.

He sat beside his mother in the waiting area, reading a comic version of one of his favourite books, *Les Misérables*. Suddenly, he became aware of two curious eyes looking at him.

An old lady was seated across his chair. Like him, she was reading, not a book but a magazine that she had taken from the pile on the receptionist's desk. But he knew she wasn't really reading because every so often she would look at him discreetly from behind the open pages. Her pointy nose reminded him of witches in storybooks on the lookout for chubby little boys to eat. Her large keen eyes moved in an untiring vigil of sorts, the same way Inspector Javert kept a close watch on the elusive Valjean.

Zeke did not like the feeling of being under scrutiny. No one does. For a boy his age, the awkwardness was overwhelming; he felt as if he couldn't breathe.

'After the check-up, we can find a good place for lunch,' said his mother, trying to sound cheerful amid the tension. She never liked check-ups; they made her nervous, which further aggravated her condition.

'What would you like to have for lunch? Burgers and fries?' she asked Zeke.

Unable to escape the old lady's field of vision, the boy felt a sense of panic. He wanted to tell his mother, or maybe just tug at her sleeve. But he was overtaken by fear and anxiety. He couldn't speak, again—his third episode of selective mutism that week. He just sat there holding the comic book, unable to speak or move.

His mother repeated the question, with a hint of exasperation, before adding, 'Oh, please don't give me another one of your episodes. I am tired of it—' her voice broke. 'I don't think I can take it any more.' She cupped her hand over her mouth in a bid to stop herself from breaking down.

The old lady overheard the conversation and said rather unabashedly, 'Young boys have their own ways of shutting out adults. Sometimes, they pretend not to hear when they are not ready with an answer.'

Zeke's mother seemed to calm down on hearing the old lady's remark. It was unsolicited but she felt relieved that another human being cared enough to talk sense into her and avert her bubble from bursting.

'When he freezes like that, I feel like I have failed him.' There were beady tears on the edge of her eyes, waiting to fall.

The old lady stood up and sat on the vacant seat next to hers.

'Maybe it was my fault. Maybe your boy got scared of me. I'm so sorry but I couldn't help but stare at him. He looks so much like my son whom I lost a long time ago.'

The old lady's honest self-admonition was unexpected. Zeke's mother started to relax as she listened to the old lady who recounted the memorable moments she had of her son who as a young man, had gone missing during the Martial Law years.

'My son, too, had a speech disorder when he was young, so I understand what you're going through. He couldn't speak until he was three or four years old. I was alarmed at first but later on, the doctor advised us not to pressure him into talking. So, we carried on normal conversations. But most of the time, he just listened as I did all the talking.' The old woman said with a chuckle.

'Then when he seemed to have gotten over it, he talked endlessly, voicing his opinion about anything and everything! He would complain about *taho* being too sweet, my *adobo* being too salty, or his playmates cheating in their games. He just couldn't stop. My ears would hurt from all his blabbering.'

Watching her talk with such profound yearning and enthusiasm made Zeke feel uneasy. Was it envy? How could he envy another boy whom he had never met? Could his mother speak about him in the same adoring way?

Meeting the old lady at the doctor's clinic became a strange but welcome encounter for Zeke. Listening to her talk about her son's similar condition made him feel less bad about himself. He wasn't alone in the world after all. He wasn't a freak because there was someone with the same condition. And this condition would soon pass. He would outgrow it, like the boy did. The old lady said so.

The old lady gave him hope. Now he had something to look forward to—the day when the attacks would cease like it did for the old lady's son so he could talk about anything that caught his eye or piqued his interest. And his mother wouldn't feel disappointed with him any more.

Looking at his mother talking to the old lady, Zeke couldn't recall the last time he had seen her look as happy. He was used to seeing her angry and frustrated every day, over his silent episodes.

Aside from anger and frustration, the sadness never left his mother's eyes. At home, Zeke had observed her sitting silently by the window, looking out, as if waiting for someone to come. Then, after an hour or two, she would draw the curtain and retire to her room but not without tears in her eyes.

Whenever he had a chance to sketch, he remembered drawing his mother's beautiful face. He would colour her cheeks pink and make her hair longer and curlier than it was. He would draw her eyes big with expectation and waiting, but her mouth was always in a straight line because he had no memory of seeing it curve upwards in a smile.

No one could smile and wait at the same time, he surmised. It took patience and a lot of perseverance to keep waiting for someone who never showed up. Her brows had a weary look, not because she was tired at the end of the day from her office job, but because her mind, no matter how exhausted, refused to give up the wait.

He knew that she hated going for her check-ups. But after meeting the old lady, he saw her smile. And the smile stayed on her lips for some time. Seeing her smile made Zeke smile too. *Things might change from here on*, he thought.

As months passed, Zeke's mother looked forward to her visits to the clinic, not to see the doctor but to see the old lady in the waiting room. Maybe because somehow she had found an ally and mentor to talk to, about how to raise a boy with a speech disorder or how to go about life as a single parent.

Ironically, around the time she began looking forward to her check-ups, she didn't need them as much any more. Her check-ups became less frequent as her condition improved—no more chest pains. It should have been a reason to be happy but the consequences were unexpected—her emotional and mental well-being suffered.

Now she needed to see another kind of doctor, a psychiatrist. Later, Zeke learnt that it was a doctor for those who couldn't stop worrying over things, causing the person to get sick from too much thinking.

It pained the young boy to see his mother looking sullen. He was young but not helpless. He knew the solution to his mother's condition was not therapy but someone with whom she could talk to about her troubles, someone who could understand her situation. She needed the old lady, her frank admonition, and her gentle and compassionate voice that somehow gave her comfort and hope while making her feel that she was not alone.

So Zeke vowed to look for the old lady in the doctor's clinic. He must find her and ask her to come see his mother. He knew she could talk sense into her. He knew the old lady could, somehow, bring his mother back to her old wistful yet cheerful self.

One day, after school, he secretly dropped by the cardiologist's clinic to sit in the waiting area to see if the old lady with a pointed nose and keen gentle eyes would come for a check-up.

'No. She hasn't come back, not even for a check-up,' said the kindly receptionist when he summed up all his courage to walk up to her and ask about the old lady's whereabouts.

Zeke felt sad and disappointed, seeing all his efforts of coming and waiting go to waste. He somewhat understood how his mother must have felt waiting for someone who never showed up.

Chapter Nine

Take a Walk and Breathe

Sometimes you need to take a walk to clear your mind. But a lot still depends on who you are walking with.

—Zechariah 'Zeke' Dipasupil

Growing up with a mother who suffered from chronic depression, chest pains, vertigo and frequent occasions of unexplained fatigue, Zeke made a vow to himself that he would devote his time and energy by assisting her in any way he could. He put himself in charge of her pill organizer, which he would bring to her after every meal, along with a glass of water, to make sure she took her medicines regularly.

He also set a reminder for all her doctor's appointments so she wouldn't miss any. He made it a point to accompany her to her check-ups and kept a handy notebook to record all the diagnoses, prescriptions and recommendations made by her doctors.

He would massage her temples whenever she was stressed from work or give her feet and ankles a good kneading when she felt tired.

He prided himself as his mother's masseuse, secretary, nurse, and overall assistant, because she had no one else to look after her. He was all she had in the world.

While Zeke worried over his mother's health condition, she seemed to have her own way of picking herself up.

One Saturday afternoon, she said, 'Let's go out for a walk.'

Zeke was only too glad to get out of the house. He wanted a change of scenery and felt that his mother needed it too, even more than he did.

A trip to the bay walk was among Zeke's favourite past times, next to reading, writing, sketching and photography.

The bay side promenade was located along Roxas Boulevard in the heart of Manila. Overlooking Manila Bay was a leisure spot, popular among bikers, tourists and families who wanted a whiff of warm salty breeze along with a majestic view of the afternoon sun just dipping low in the horizon. The bay walk also acted as a seawall.

The entire stretch of the bay walk, all two kilometres of it, had its own charm—open-air cafés, restaurants offering various cuisines, live band music, street performances, and boats offering night cruises.

The sprawling Mall of Asia, the premier shopping centre of the SM Group of Companies, was also within walking distance from the bay walk. Anyone visiting, whether for peace and quiet near the sea or a dining or shopping adventure, would definitely find the trip rewarding.

The sea offered a certain kind of solace for the weary, while the bustling establishments around it provided sustenance and leisure for the restless.

In the kitchen, Zeke saw his mother preparing some sandwiches while humming a happy tune, anticipating their outing with newfound eagerness. She had also packed some chips from the cupboard and grabbed some cold soda drinks from the fridge for the trip.

'Other than the snacks, I have also packed the picnic mat so we can sit on the seawall. You can bring along your camera and a book if you want,' she said.

Zeke packed his trusted DSLR, sketch pad and pencil. He would sometimes draw if inspiration hit him. But on days when he lacked the patience to draw or if the wind was blowing too hard, he would just take snapshots. It was easier and quicker, even though lacking in the emotional department.

He also took along his favourite illustrated copy of *Les Miserables* by the French romantic novelist Victor Hugo. He liked it so much he could read it over and over again.

There was something about the novel that appealed to him, particularly the characters leading sad, wretched but not entirely hopeless lives. He could identify with them, alone and miserable, different from the rest of the crowd—like a freak as some of his classmates labelled him—struggling not to wallow in grief and wanting to escape from the muck.

He admired the novel's protagonist, Jean Valjean, an ex-convict who was given a second chance to live a righteous life under a new identity. But Valjean couldn't escape his past because the chief-of-police, Inspector Javert, was out to uncover his real identity.

Talk about a person trying to turn away from his evil ways and start anew, only to have someone dampen his hopes and ruin his attempts at reforming his life. How unfortunate to be judged according to one's past, that no matter how hard one tries, the good deeds cannot be reparation for past wrongdoings.

The novel became his daily companion and a refuge of sorts. The success of Jean Valjean as a new man under an assumed identity inspired him. Who could have predicted that an ex-con like Valjean could reform his life, own a factory, and even be elected as the town mayor?

For Zeke, a man's past should not dictate his future. He felt that everyone is always given a choice between good and evil, to follow the easy but crooked road or create an entirely new path away from the old.

As he re-read the novel, he was also searching for clues to figure out what he wanted to be in the future—unlike most of his classmates, Zeke had not yet figured this out. He asked himself some question: How did Valjean know that he wanted to become a businessman and own a factory? How did he know that the townsfolk would elect him as mayor? From a nobody to somebody, it was a good career path to take.

Zeke thought that it would be easier for him to know what he wanted if he had known his father. He would have really liked to have model to follow, an example to emulate.

'Who am I really?' Zeke had asked himself a couple of times in front of the bathroom mirror. 'Who is my father? What kind of man is he? Is he worth emulating?'

Zeke wanted so much to know about his father because he couldn't deny that his father was part of his life—a vital part that was missing.

But not everyone has their wishes or prayers answered the way they want. Zeke's mother seldom talked about his father, like he was a part of her past that she would rather leave behind. But despite this, Zeke found consolation that all would be revealed at the proper time. It said so in the novel.

So, for now, he was content sitting on a good spot near the sea next to his mother, munching on a sandwich, sipping cold soda, and watching the waves make soft lapping sounds on the rocks that lined the shoreline below.

The trip to the bay walk was indeed a great idea. The sound of the water, the smell of the sea, and the sight of the rare migratory birds were all recorded in his brain as part of a memorable and pleasurable experience he would cherish all his life.

'Look, Ma! Birds!' Zeke exclaimed upon spotting several egrets flying low. Quickly, he got his camera and took a few shots of the birds that looked like white flags flapping in the wind.

'Aren't they beautiful?' She smiled in appreciation.

'Ma, did you also come here when you were young?' Zeke dared to ask his mother, hoping she would give him a glimpse of her past.

She looked intently at Zeke then looked away, her brows scrunched together like she was in deep thought.

Zeke waited in eager anticipation—his heart racing, his lips whispering a prayer that she wouldn't drop the topic.

Finally, she spoke, 'I used to come here with your father.'

Zeke froze hearing her words. He felt panic because his chest had no air; it was like he had momentarily forgotten what it was like to breathe.

'What was he like?' Zeke managed to ask. He was hoping their conversation would go on, unlike in the past when she would shift her thoughts to another topic.

'I recall walking with him ... telling him how beautiful the sea is and how it calms my nerves ... but he doesn't seem to hear me.'

When his mother fell silent, Zeke decided to ask again, 'Why is that?'

His mother shrugged her shoulders. 'All I know is that he was worried about so many things ... and he was thinking of what he could do to make things better.'

Hearing his mother talk about the father he had never met made Zeke recall the yearning that had haunted him in his sleep—how he had dreamt about a shadow of a man carrying him high on his shoulders. But the man's face was blank, like a phantom's. He would wake up sobbing. It was like a piece of a puzzle that was missing in his life. He felt like he would never really feel complete.

Suddenly, his thoughts were interrupted; Zeke felt like he was being watched. There was something in the air that made his hair stand on end. It was almost the same feeling as when he was in the waiting area at the doctor's clinic and noticed the old lady secretly observing him.

The bay walk was a large public area so it was a strange assumption to make, since there was a lot of movement around them—from people sitting on picnic mats to vendors roaming around selling their wares.

Looking around, Zeke tried to find an 'odd man out' among the people strolling, biking, jogging or sitting on mats. Some people were taking pictures. Some were sitting in groups and others by their lonesome selves. Still others were silently watching the sun take a dip in the horizon, creating a masterpiece in the sky before darkness set in.

Zeke felt anxious. He never liked the feeling of being scrutinized. He looked in another direction hoping to see something out of the ordinary.

Then, he noticed a man sitting at the far end of the seawall. He was a bit old, maybe around sixty, wearing a fishing hat and dimmed glasses as if to hide his eyes.

The overcast sky added to his dismal mood, and a gust of cold wind completed the formula for fear to set in.

'Mama, I think there's someone watching us,' Zeke told his mother in a soft, casual voice, trying not to sound alarmed.

'Why would someone be watching us?' his mother retorted. 'We're not celebrities or secret agents. Maybe you've been watching too many movies,' she added, dismissing his fears.

Zeke tried not to look directly at the man. Observing him from his peripheral view, he saw that the man brought out a newspaper and started reading. Then he saw him hold a small device that looked like a camera and began taking snaps in their direction, very discreetly from behind the newspaper.

'Mama, I don't like the way the man was acting. Seems like he's taking a photo of us.'

'Nonsense,' his mother whispered back, trying to see the man. 'But if you don't feel comfortable, we can pack and go home.

There's no point staying here if it makes you anxious. We don't want another anxiety attack.'

Zeke nodded in agreement. He was feeling the tension rise up to his throat. He grabbed his things in haste and stuffed them inside his bag. His mother also began packing up.

Suddenly, grey clouds formed in thick clusters overhead. Not long after, a light shower began to fall.

People who were reclining on picnic blankets and relaxing on the seawall quickly got up and rushed to find shelter to keep themselves from getting wet.

Zeke's mother held his hand as they ran to a nearby café and took shelter underneath its bright pink canopies. There were several others too, all taking shelter underneath the giant umbrella-like structures.

'Glad we made it,' Zeke's mother muttered in relief.

'Couldn't agree more,' said a man. 'Wouldn't want to get wet in this weather.'

Zeke turned in the direction of the voice. Then he froze in fear. It was the same man who had been watching them. He could be mistaken, but this man was wearing the same fishing hat and the same round smoked glasses.

As the shower turned into a downpour, Zeke wanted to warn his mother about the man, that they should at least take a few steps away from him without getting noticed.

But he couldn't talk. Fear and anxiety were building up, making it difficult for him to breathe.

A lot of what-ifs began to form in his head:

What if the man is a robber and suddenly pulls out a gun or a knife?
What if his mother defends him against the man and gets stabbed or shot?
What if nobody helps them? How will he get his mother to a hospital?
What if his mother dies from a stab or gunshot wound?
Who is this man anyway?
What does he want from us?

Zeke tugged at his mother's sleeve desperately. He was trying to form words in his mouth, but all he could say was 'ma … ma … '.

His mother sensing her son's anxiety, hugged him closer to her side and whispered, 'It's okay, Zeke. It's okay. The rain will stop, and we'll be home soon.'

Chapter Ten

A Boy Unlike His Father

Love is a strange thing. It makes you do things you never thought you could do on your own. But when it's gone, it makes you see the weaknesses you never thought you had.

—Zeke's mother

His name was John Alexander. We met in college. I was a junior student while he was in his senior year. We were an unlikely pair. I was a barrio lass, ignorant to the ways of the world, subsisting on a meagre allowance that my parents sent me every week. He was a boy from Manila—smart and confident. He belonged to a middle-class family that owned a small eating place in the city. His father was a retired OFW who started a food business.

My father was a farmer who believed in hard work to feed his family of six. I couldn't say John Alexander's father worked any less hard as a businessman running their small eating joint. We were both raised by two good men who worked long hours to provide a good life for their families.

John Alexander would invite me for afternoon snacks at the college cafeteria where we enjoyed eating banana que and kwek-kwek.

'Is it a yes?' John Alexander had asked me for the nth time. He wanted to marry me right after college. I loved him but I was unsure if my parents would allow me to do so. I felt my parents would have wanted me to get a job after graduation and help put my other siblings through school.

'I don't know.' I hung my head every time he popped the question.

We kept our relationship a secret. We tried not to show any display of affection on campus. We wanted people to think that we were just very good friends. I felt that I wasn't yet ready to reveal our relationship to my friends. I didn't want the news to reach my parents and get them worried that I might not finish my studies.

The following year, he asked me the big question again. I refused to give him an answer until I was sure my name was on the list of graduating students. Besides, it wasn't a good time to start a family.

There was growing public unrest because of the crisis in the economy. Oil prices were rising, along with the prices of basic commodities. Wage earners were putting lesser and lesser food on the table. Student activism was rampant. Young people, with their brilliant idealism and exuberant spirit, were clamouring for change in a society under a government that refused to listen to the cries of the people.

Oh, how we loved to gather in assemblies and listen to student leaders standing atop parked vehicles, addressing the crowd until their voices cracked. They spoke about the plight of the working class, the farmers and labourers, the poor and the voiceless.

Listening to those powerful voices, we felt their hurt, fear, anger and frustrations. We were transformed from being curious bystanders into men and women who believed that they could bring about the change they wished to see by voicing their thoughts and demanding a better future for their children and their children's children.

Soon, after joining one protest rally after another, we stopped being afraid. We were drawn to the student rallies demanding rollbacks in tuition fees because it hurt our parent's pockets. It pained us to see our parents worry that our allowances might not last us for a week.

Thereafter, we joined rallies against the dormitory fee increase. We demanded student consultations and dialogues before the implementation of the price increase.

We raised our placards higher and made our voices louder. Soon, even the college deans and the university president himself joined the dialogue to listen to our demands. We felt jubilant that our voices were heard.

But we had no idea that the small rallies we found ourselves swimming in would lead to bigger waves that would unwittingly sweep us into larger assemblies on topics that were outside the university and more national in scope. From a small stream, we were taken in by the rushing tide. And there was no stopping the rivulets from finding their way to the sea.

We joined the angry mob of student activists by marching into the streets, demanding to end the oppression of the poor and the violation of human rights. Sometimes the protests were loud and violent. There were improvised bombs or pillbox bombs that the protesters hurled at policemen trying to disperse them.

On one instance, I saw a pillbox bomb come from the ranks of the police. It was strange. I felt the policemen themselves wanted the protest rallies to become violent for them to justify their actions to arrest and detain whomever they could get their hands on.

We saw some student activists being taken forcibly into custody by police or army personnel then later released a few days later, almost half-dead. The police said they wanted it to serve as a warning for the others. But it only made things worse. The violent arrests and police brutality fuelled more rallies as more and more people took to the streets.

John Alexander and I had agreed that if the worst befell us, we would escape arrest by running in opposite directions and meet up again at his mother's eatery, Conchita's. Luckily, that never happened since the protest rallies we participated in were calm and organized.

By the time we reached our final semester, I saw the change in John Alexander. He had become a different man. Though he loved me, his heart belonged elsewhere, moved as he was by a higher calling to create a better society. He got more involved in the protest movements with other student activists. Rallies and public outcries took place left and right. Students were no longer in the classrooms but on the streets. It was a tumultuous period in Philippine history, now labelled as First Quarter Storm.

John Alexander and I had planned on getting married the following year after graduation. I had already told my parents about his intention to marry me. I was sure and certain that he wanted me to be his wife. I saw the certainty in his eyes when he asked me to marry him, over and over again.

'Will you marry me, be my wife and the mother of my children?' John Alexander asked.

'Y-E-S!'

Marrying John Alexander was the next best thing after earning my degree. I wanted to finish college not so much for myself but for my parents who worked hard to see that I got a good education. It was every parent's dream after all, to set their children out into the world with a strong moral foundation, faith in God, confidence in one's abilities, and most importantly, armed with a college diploma.

But the vision to marry became clouded with the more pressing concerns of daily life. And as weeks passed, things never really cleared up. There was no date, no church, no clear direction about the wedding. I only knew John Alexander wanted to marry me. And I said yes. But after that, there was nothing. No more talks about the wedding. So whenever my parents would ask about our wedding plans, I couldn't give them a straight answer.

Then one day, I woke up feeling sick. My head hurt, and I felt queasy. I told John Alexander I couldn't attend my class because my head was throbbing like crazy. He told me to take a painkiller and rest in the dormitory. He would just tell my professors and ask that I be excused for being sick. He kissed me on the head and promised to come in the afternoon and bring me dinner.

That night, he brought me my favourite chicken and pork adobo with boiled egg and rice wrapped in banana leaf, locally known as *binalot* from the Filipino word meaning 'wrapped'. It was my all-time favourite comfort food but that day when I saw the food on the table, I didn't feel like eating it. My taste buds were off. My olfactory nerves had gone awry. In fact, I was appalled by the aroma of black pepper and bay leaf in the adobo.

Still, we ate together at the dormitory's cafeteria. Every bite I took was painful, but since I didn't want to offend him or make a scene, I tried to wash down every spoonful with a gulp of water, hoping he wouldn't notice. He didn't. Instead, he spoke in high spirits, telling me excitedly about his day. He barely noticed that I wasn't eating much. After each spoonful, I felt like I was about to throw up.

He then proceeded to narrate how he got an invitation, along with the other student leaders, from government representatives for a dialogue. Their group had reasons to believe their protests were being heard and would soon be addressed by the government.

I wanted so badly to tell him how my day went, that I took a pregnancy test and the test came out positive. I wanted to tell him that we would become parents very soon.

But seeing him talk endlessly about the many sleepless nights they had spent planning their protest plans, printing flyers and leaflets and collaborating with other groups who share the same sentiment, I became hesitant.

An important dialogue with the government had been set. He needed to focus his energy on that meeting. The last thing he needed was a distraction. And I wouldn't want to give him that. I loved him too much that I dared not stand in the way of his aspirations to finally get the reforms he so desperately sought for our family and the society as a whole.

I kept the joyful news to myself. I told myself it could wait a few more days or maybe a week until the meeting with the government was over.

I had told John Alexander about my fear of him being arrested, of sharing the fate of those whose luck had run out. I told him that we did not know the day or the hour when a life would be given and when a life would be taken away.

But he said he wasn't afraid to die because a life without a purpose was a life not worth living. And that we lived not for the sake of our own selves but also for others.

My fears came true when John Alexander and his fellow activists failed to return after their meeting with government representatives. No one knew where they were, if they were imprisoned, or tortured or dead.

Weeks after their meeting on 21 September 1972, Martial Law was signed by then President Ferdinand E. Marcos. The declaration was justified given the violence on the streets and mounting civil unrest. The military that had reported its officers in uniform were wounded by violent protesters during dispersals was given full control to keep the peace.

Along with the declaration was the suspension of the Writ of Habeas Corpus. Human rights were suspended, including freedom of speech and assembly. News and media companies were closed down. News and information were closely monitored and limited to only those authorized by the government to be released.

Nobody knew what had become of John Alexander and his fellow student activists. All my enquiries just led to a dead end.

Even the families of his companions had given up hope of ever seeing them again.

I cried silent tears at night with only my unborn child as my witness. I did not know whom to turn to. I dared not tell my parents about my condition. I feared the shame of having a child out of wedlock. So I decided to raise my son on my own. I told them I had eloped and asked for their forgiveness and understanding.

I knew I wasn't thinking clearly during those times. But who would after losing a friend, a lover, the father of their child, and the one who was fighting for a better society. I could still hear his voice in my dreams, loud and shrill, asking to stop the abuses of those in power, demanding for justice, for equal rights, for fair labour practices for the working class, for increase in salaries and benefits, to give what is due, and to give peace and freedom a chance. But his voice was ignored and silenced too soon.

Fourteen years later, the dictatorship ended not by the might of armies but by a bloodless and peaceful revolution known the world over as the EDSA People Power Revolution.

Many believed it was made possible by the Hand that created the universe, as majority of the people were devout Catholics. Prayers could indeed move mountains, lay down guns, tear down thrones and monuments, and topple governments. No one could have predicted the miracle to happen amid the chaos, as it was unlikely for a flower to bloom in an arid land like the desert. Alas, John Alexander wasn't there to witness the birth of a new society where there was freedom, where his son would flourish and grow.

And just like that, my baby boy was born without a father. He came out into the world crying but his voice was just a whimper. He was curly-haired like a cherub with a big, round chest and equally large arms and legs. He had a bad temper. He had frequent tantrums, like he was angry with the world, and condoling with my grief and loss.

I named him Zechariah, after the father of John the Baptist, from the Bible. I liked the sound of Zeke as a nickname. To me, it sounded hip and cool.

I imagined my boy to grow up confident and boisterous like his father, whose commanding voice would reverberate in halls and capture the minds and hearts of anyone willing to listen.

But fate had a different plan because my boy did not care to make a sound at all. He seemed to have a speech delay and was voiceless until he was four years old. I thought it was my fault for naming him after a biblical character who was punished to become mute because of his unbelief.

In the days of Herod, King of Judea, there was a priest named Zechariah of the priestly division of Abijah; his wife was from the daughters of Aaron, and her name was Elizabeth. But they had no child, because Elizabeth was barren and both were advanced in years.

Then, when the whole assembly of the people was praying outside at the hour of the incense offering, the angel of the Lord appeared to him, standing at the right of the altar of incense. Zechariah was troubled by what he saw, and fear came upon him.

But the angel said to him, 'Do not be afraid, Zechariah, because your prayer has been heard. Your wife Elizabeth will bear you a son, and you shall name him John.'

Then Zechariah said to the angel, 'How shall I know this? For I am an old man, and my wife is advanced in years.' And the angel said to him in reply, 'I am Gabriel, who stand before God. I was sent to speak to you and to announce to you this good news. But now you will be speechless and unable to talk until the day these things take place, because you did not believe my words, which will be fulfilled at their proper time.' (Luke 1: 5, 10–13, 18–20)

My boy Zechariah, or 'Zeke', was gentle, quiet, and well-behaved. He would play noiselessly with his toy cars and fire trucks. And whenever I would call out to him to come and eat at the dining table with me, he would smile and nod back. He resembled his father in many ways, except that he was voiceless, choosing to express his feelings and thoughts through gestures.

'Your child has selective mutism,' said the doctor who diagnosed him. 'He might be stressed out by unfamiliar situations or people around him. It is best to observe what things or circumstances cause his anxiety.'

Chapter Eleven

The Art of Losing

Sometimes we get angry when people say the things we don't want to hear. But it happens for a reason—not because they find pleasure by saying it but because we need to hear it.

—Des

Mr Zultan felt edgy as he sat on the large leather armchair by his desk. He couldn't believe he had just fired his most brilliant editor over one petty argument.

'Define petty,' he told himself. 'How petty is petty?' he asked himself again, incredulous at what just happened at the editors' budget meeting. 'And by whose standards?'

Now he had lost his best man on the job. Zeke was among the most brilliant journalists he had ever met—smart, fair, zealously in love with the truth.

He had interviewed the young man when he was applying for a job as a field reporter many years back.

Zeke got the highest score on the aptitude test among thirty aspirants who showed up that day. Zultan wanted to interview the top three candidates. He wanted to see them in person, get to know their quirks and personalities, their biases and views on the world. Not that he wanted them to share the same view as his, but he wanted to see if they could express it without any fear, doubt, or hesitation.

The other two, a man and a woman, arrived early, smartly dressed; one in a black pin-striped coat and the other in a cream-white blazer. Zeke arrived a while later wearing a coat that was not too dark but in a shade of ashen grey.

Zultan asked them if they were aware of the current issues: corruption scandals and the electoral fraud besetting the then President Macapagal-Arroyo, the planned amendment of the constitution to allow for a parliamentary form of government, the longstanding armed insurgencies in the south, etc.

Then, he asked them, 'If you were the adviser, what advice would you give the President?'

The other two gave short and safe answers. Their replies were acceptable but did not leave a mark, whereas Zeke expressed his honest opinion on things, whether the person in front of him would agree or not. He didn't even look bothered when Zultan looked displeased at what he was hearing.

'I'd tell the President that scandals create questions in the mind of the people about her character and integrity as an elected official. I would suggest stepping down as the proper thing to do in the name of *delicadeza*. It's best to make a graceful and honourable exit.'

Zultan sniggered upon hearing his answer. 'You got nerves of steel, boy, to tell that to the President. But I'm not too sure if she would accept that and let you keep your job.'

Zeke thought for a moment then looked straight at Zultan, his eyes unfazed. 'Sir, it's my job to tell the President the best plan of action, whether she likes it or not, whether I lose my job or not.'

Zultan couldn't deny that he was impressed with the young man's line of thinking. But he also felt afraid because the young man's boldness to proclaim the truth might have grave consequences.

During the last part of the interview, Zultan wanted to test Zeke by asking for his opinion on the Hacienda Luisita Massacre, which had been all over the news for weeks. Several picketing farmers including two children were killed and more than a hundred were injured and arrested when police and soldiers tried to disperse a blockade by plantation workers at the sugar estate. The farmers were asking for an increase in their wages and benefits, and more broadly, demanding the land due to them under the Agrarian Reform programme of the government.

'So, who do you think should be held accountable for the incident? The person who pulled the trigger? The person who gave the order? Or the owners of the hacienda?' Zultan asked again.

'It's always easy to point a finger when we're not personally involved in the incident. Land dispute is a serious issue because the Philippines is an agricultural economy. It's sad to see how we treat the poor, the weak and the helpless like they have less rights than the privileged. The police should be held accountable because they should have only arrested and detained the protesters, but they crossed the line when they shot at the protesters. The persons who authorized the dispersal also have a share in the accountability. But since the issue is still under investigation, it's too early to judge.'

Zultan liked the way Zeke responded to his questions—straightforward but not too quick to pass judgement. A good journalist would always tell a story from a balanced perspective. Add to that his commitment to seek the truth.

He also admired the way Zeke regarded him with respect, like that of a colleague and not exuding fear like the other applicants.

In the end, he had chosen Zeke for the job because he was an unbiased, hard-hitting and fearless truth-seeker.

But now, this hard-hitting truth-seeker had turned against him. He was raging like a bull to get his way.

For Zultan, the front page was not something anyone else could mess with. It was off limits for anyone but Zultan. It was the face and voice of the news agency, his territory, his seat of power.

So when Zeke attempted to persuade him and the other editors to put an article on the front page, hurling insults as he did, Zultan was extremely offended. He was not the person who would take insults sitting down. So he dropped him.

The news editor post is an important position in any news agency. And so is the managing director's post. Zeke occupied both, so his intelligence, capability, and aptitude weren't easy to match. Zultan knew that it would probably take months before a replacement could be found. Even then, he doubted if he would find someone as good as this man, whom he had just thrown out like a free meal for other news agencies to grab. He wouldn't be surprised if Zeke gets a job offer from rival agencies within the next hour.

Zeke lost his job, but it was a great loss to the company too. Now who's on the losing side? For real?

* * *

The next morning, Zultan arrived at the office earlier than usual. As he passed by his secretary's desk, he barked, 'Give me a copy of that damn article!'

'Which article are you referring to, Sir?' Des, his secretary, asked.

'The article about the dead drug runner that Mr Dipasupil exchanged his job for!'

'Oh, did you just fire him over some petty article, Sir?' His secretary couldn't help but ask.

Zultan was exasperated. 'If you poke your nose into things that don't concern you, you might lose your job too!'

'Oh, I'm sorry, Sir. I'll get you a copy ASAP!'

He had never liked his secretary's nosy attitude. On several instances, irked by her lack of tact, he had already made up his mind to fire her. But at the end of the day, he would change his mind because her bubbly personality, candour and efficiency at work always got in the way. Not to mention his office looked more alive, and his day felt right whenever he saw the bright pink bow on her head. More so, her tendency to throw in a question out of curiosity sometimes served a good purpose. It jolted him to rethink the consequences of his actions and decisions.

As soon as his secretary handed him the article, he cleared his desk of any loose papers, put on his round spectacles and read the article earnestly, word by word, line by line.

The article was written by a junior field reporter.

Boy, dead at 14, tagged as drug runner

22 November 2016. Caloocan City, Metro Manila. Fourteen-year-old Eliseo 'Jun-Jun' Reyes, Jr was among the latest casualties in the government's anti-drug campaign. He was accidentally shot on Friday night by anti-drug operatives of the Caloocan police district after allegedly trying to elude a peaceful arrest.

According to Police Inspector Arnulfo Tobias Dela Cruz, they went to the victim's apartment inside a compound on J.P. Rizal Street to conduct a peaceful 'knock and plead' negotiation under the Oplan Tokhang programme. It is short for Operational Plan Tuktok Hangyo, the anti-illegal drugs campaign launched by the government that aims to help those involved in drugs to quit the drug habit and reform their lives.

The boy, a scholar at Caloocan City's Science High School, was believed to be working covertly as a drug runner. His name was on the police intelligence drug watch list.

The boy was asked to go with the police for questioning but was reported to have attempted to run away. The police made some warning shots in an attempt to prevent the boy from escaping but the boy was accidentally hit.

The boy was taken to the nearby Caloocan City General Hospital but died soon after.

'It was an accidental shooting. They were warning shots meant to stop the boy. We never meant to harm him,' said Police Inspector Dela Cruz.

Eliseo 'Jun-Jun' Reyes, Jr had lost his father in a construction accident. He is survived by his siblings, Angelo and Princess, and his mother, Benilda, who works as a domestic helper abroad.

'We are saddened that the drug problem has indeed become doubly dangerous for our young people. We condole with the family on this unfortunate incident,' concluded Dela Cruz.

The Philippine National Police (PNP) will extend burial assistance to the family of the deceased.

Zultan laid the article on his desk but his mind was racing. How many other similar articles had he read and approved for publishing in the past week? In the past months? There were just too many. Should he be alarmed? Maybe. The rising number of casualties simply couldn't be ignored any more. He thought maybe Zeke had a point. This culture of death was spreading unbelievably fast like fire, reaching even the children who were supposedly safe inside their homes. How do you sound the alarm as a warning when your house is already burning?

He could still recall when Oplan Tokhang was first rolled out by the Philippine National Police after former Davao City Mayor Rodrigo Duterte became President. It was the biggest story on the front page, which they ran for a month or so. The word 'Tokhang' had become a common word, spoken on the streets and at home by both young and old. It became a source of fear, a subject of dread for many—or a joke to some. It became an excuse for parents to remind their children to come home early or else be killed—*Baka ma-tokhang ka*, where 'tokhang' was used as a verb synonymous with 'kill'. The drug issue just wasn't meant to be taken lightly.

The operational plan involved police officers and local barangay officials visiting the houses of suspected drug addicts and drug pushers to persuade and warn them to stop their illegal activities or move out. Alternately, they could also avail of the government's drug rehabilitation and livelihood programme to turn away from their illegal trade.

The crackdown against illegal drugs was meant to be a peaceful negotiation without using coercion, threat or violence. But with the growing number of casualties, the reality was far from peaceful.

Zultan looked out the window after reading the article. A boy's life had stopped but life went on for the others, as was evident from the busy intersection outside his window. People were going about their usual day, minding their own business. No one had stopped to notice that one boy was gone too soon. Only his family would miss him. Perhaps his classmates and teachers too. But not the rest of the world. No one cared because no one knew. And this series of senseless killings could go on if nobody cared enough to bring it to the light.

'Can you call Mr Dipasupil?' Zultan asked his secretary, his voice lower than usual with undertones of regret. 'And please tell him to come to my office.'

'Right away, Sir!' came Des's reply, in the same perky high-pitched voice.

After a few rings, she reported back. 'Sir, he's not answering his phone. I think maybe because he doesn't work here any more? You fired him—'

'I know what I did!'

He couldn't bear to hear his mistake blasted straight to his face. 'You keep your damn opinion to yourself. Just get his ass in here!'

* * *

Meanwhile, Zeke hardly got any sleep. The scene at the meeting room kept replaying in his mind. He couldn't believe that he had screamed at his boss the night before, and his hands still hurt after slamming the table so hard.

After the rage came the frustration, then the regret. Now he was feeling rather sentimental. He needed to go back to the office early to clear his desk. He didn't want to accidentally bump into Mr Zultan. It would be best to leave as discreetly as possible and let the wounds heal.

He would definitely miss a lot of things. He would miss the Everglade Tower and its green oasis rooftop. He would miss Rey and their secret dialogue at the reception area. He would miss barking at delinquent reporters telling them to mind their deadlines. He would miss the late-night budget meetings with the editors, and probably Mr Zultan too, his mentor who had taught him many things and served as a father figure to him.

Going back to the office, he was surprised to find Roy so early at his desk.

'I heard about what happened last night … ' Roy started, looking sullen. 'I thought I'd catch you before you go.'

For a while, Zeke couldn't find an appropriate response. He was touched by Roy's gesture and felt that he deserved an explanation. He just didn't know how to start. He stood motionless at the door, his feet refusing to follow his bidding.

Seeing Roy looking sad and hurt to see him leave made him feel guilty. He realized now the consequences of his actions would affect not just himself but also others like Roy, who would be burdened by the work he would leave behind.

'People had been chatting non-stop in my group. You've become a star overnight.'

They both chuckled awkwardly.

'You wouldn't want to be in my shoes,' Zeke said. In his mind, as a journalist, he had been telling the news for so long. Now he found himself at the other end of the spectrum as news fodder, and nothing came close to describing the feeling.

The meeting scenario played again in his mind, and he felt he could have averted the situation if he had just controlled his temper.

'I don't know what has gotten into me. I totally lost my cool in there. Couldn't blame Mr Z for giving me the pink slip for shouting at him.' Zeke said with a sigh. He felt he could have done better. Just then, Zeke's phone rang. There was a woman on the other end of the line. It was Des. Her voice sounded urgent, telling him to go to Mr Zultan's office immediately.

'That was weird. Why does Mr Zultan want to see me this early?' Zeke wondered out loud.

'Do you think he changed his mind?' asked Roy, looking hopeful.

Zeke shook his head. 'Knowing the old man, I doubt it. He seldom retracts what he said.'

'Maybe you could at least apologize before you go,' suggested Roy. 'Never burn your bridges, as they say.'

Zeke thought for a moment about what Roy had said. 'You got a point there,' he said as he grabbed his jacket and flew out the door, a stark contrast to his legs that wouldn't budge a few minutes ago.

* * *

Zultan's office was located on the floor above the editorial offices.

Zeke decided to take the stairs. His legs could use the extra movement to keep his blood circulating and pump enough oxygen into his brain to keep it functioning properly. Also he knew he had to ensure that this time there wouldn't be a shouting match.

As he stepped out of the lift and walked towards Zultan's office, he couldn't remember the last time he had been here. Most interactions with Zultan were done over phone or email.

The entire area appeared cold and dark, giving it a sombre quality. Was it the black interiors or the absence of paintings or sculptures or anything to hint at life, freshness or vibrancy? But overall, it still lived up to the character of the news agency's most powerful man.

Then he noticed a bright pink bow that stood out from the dull scenery. It was on top of the head of a lady who appeared to be Zultan's secretary.

Her workstation was brightly lit. There were also splashes of colour from her array of potted plants such as a white peace lily, a heartleaf philodendron, a dwarf yellow bamboo, and a reddish pink flowering cactus. The plants refreshed Zeke's eyes and somewhat reduced the tension he was feeling.

'Hi!' he greeted the lady. 'I'm here to see Mr Zultan.'

'Oh, hi!' the lady greeted back. 'I'm his new secretary. My name's Desiree. You can call me Des.'

Zeke extended his hand to Des. 'I'm Zeke Dipasupil. Glad to meet you, Des.'

Bubbly and high-spirited, Des was a stark contrast to the dark and sombre office. She seemed to be delighted to see another human being in the office that was almost always deserted.

'If you recall, we talked earlier on the phone. Mr Zultan was very anxious to see you. You may go in when you're ready.'

After three taps on the large, heavy door, Zeke heard his boss's familiar voice, which sounded more like an animal's grunt.

'Good morning, Sir,' Zeke greeted the old man, who was sitting on his desk with his back turned away.

'Please take a seat,' Zultan replied.

'First of all, I want to say sorry,' Zeke said as he sat down on the velvety cushion of a chair.

'I'm sorry too,' Zultan said, almost simultaneously, as he swivelled his chair around to face Zeke.

Both were surprised at the other's words of apology. Both felt the awkwardness of the situation that neither could find the words to say right after.

Zultan broke the silence.

'I read the article of contention again. A child's death is always sad and unfortunate not only for his family but also for the rest of humanity. After reading it a couple of times, I realized it's not just an incident of a young person dying. There is much more than that. It's something we cannot simply turn a blind eye on. We cannot let it pass without telling the world.'

Zeke felt relieved to hear those words. He felt light, knowing he did the right thing.

'Thank you, Sir,' Zeke said, expressing his gratitude with a humble smile.

'Don't thank me yet,' Zultan answered. 'To give due respect to our process of article selection, I've convened the editors early this morning to take an online poll. They can do it remotely from where they are. The other five are already waiting online. Let's cast our votes if this article truly deserves to be the front story for the next issue.'

One by one, the editors cast their votes. Four were in favour of putting the article on the front page. Two voted against it. One decided to abstain. In the end, Zeke left Zultan's office with a huge smile on his face but not without a gruff reminder from his boss, who was happy to have him back.

'Give me a damn good headline that will make heads turn and make sure this is worth all the trouble!'

Chapter Twelve

Waiting and Hoping

If you go through life waiting for something or somebody, it is like riding a train and missing the beautiful view outside.

—Kit Dimalanta

It was Friday night at Conchita's twenty-four-hour Bar and Grill. Kit arrived early to meet Zeke for their regular get-together at the end of the week, to unwind over a few drinks.

Zeke had messaged her earlier that he had just had a rollercoaster of events in the office and would be running a bit late. Two hours max was his promise.

'What's another two hours?' she told herself, 'when I have been practically waiting for him all my life.'

Conchita's was their favourite place to hang out because it served the best sizzling pork *sisig* in town. She liked to eat them with a bottle of ice-cold beer alongside Zeke's ginger ale. Since Conchita's was also owned by Zeke's grandmother, they benefitted from a discount too.

Zeke was a very good friend and her total opposite—he was quiet and meek while she was tough, brazen, and outspoken. Their friendship dated back to their elementary days when they sat next to each other in class since their seats were arranged alphabetically according to their last names—Dimalanta and Dipasupil.

Growing up, she had watched her friend deal with an anxiety disorder that caused him to lose his ability to speak. She knew he looked stupid when he was unable to answer during recitations, and some of their classmates would laugh or mock him secretly. She couldn't blame them because they were just kids. After all, it is normal for kids to laugh at something they find funny or amusing. Considering laughing as offensive came much later, as an afterthought for those who were sensitive to the feelings of others.

Kit remembered vividly the look of frustration on his face, how he wished he could control the attacks that made him stutter or sometimes become completely voiceless like a statue. But he was helpless against it, and he hated himself for it.

Because of this, Kit made it a point to stand by his side as much as she could. If Zeke couldn't speak, then she would be his voice—that is, until the incident.

* * *

'Any more submissions?' The teacher addressed the class one time.

'Yes, Miss! One more!' Kit called out.

'You've already submitted your paper if I'm not mistaken, Miss Dimalanta,' replied the teacher sternly.

'There's one more, Ma'am. Zeke is just finishing up.'

'Oh,' said the teacher. 'I didn't know you have a spokesperson, Mister Dipasupil. Better hurry up!'

Zeke had felt embarrassed with the entire class fixing their eyes on him.

After class, Zeke hurried to catch Kit before she stepped onto the school bus.

'Kit, thank you for speaking up for me. If you didn't, I might have failed to submit my paper on time.'

Kit was beaming. 'Anything to help a friend.'

'But please … just don't do that all the time.' Zeke had a serious look on his face.

'What kind of a request is that?' Kit looked incredulous. 'If I didn't, the teacher wouldn't have waited for your submission and you would have been marked late.'

'Just don't. You have no idea how embarrassing it is,' Zeke said as he walked away.

Kit was hurt, but for the nth time, but she wouldn't dare to share her feelings with Zeke because he was her friend. She understood perfectly that sometimes, Zeke said the wrong things without meaning to. Even later, as a journalist and an editor, Zeke was good with the written word, but alas, not so much with the spoken word. Besides, he had a terrible temper and was seldom able to control his seething words that had hurt her many times. As they matured from teenagers into adults, Zeke didn't seem to outgrow his blunt nature and occasional lack of tact.

* * *

Kit's thoughts were interrupted as she saw Zeke gingerly walking in her direction.

'Hey!' Zeke greeted her.

'You're late, as always,' Kit muttered.

'My bad. I told you I'll be running late. You should at least be happy that I got my job back,' Zeke replied.

Kit smiled looking at Zeke. She could have given him a congratulatory hug, but she dared not. She wouldn't want to feel the electricity soaring again if he came too close.

Kit had always admired Zeke because he was smart, funny, and had a big heart to help those who needed it. But as their friendship progressed, she silently wished he could look at her differently—maybe more than just a friend.

They were both in their forties, busy growing their careers, happy and carefree being single—or so they said.

Zeke had always wanted to be a journalist. In school, he was the class secretary, always writing and keeping a record of class activities. Meanwhile, she had been elected as class president because of her firm demeanour and outspokenness.

After graduating from high school, she entered the police academy, while he entered the seminary. They lost communication after that. She had earned medals for her courage and active service in the community, as a volunteer for the city's fire station. Later, she found herself in a supervisory position and was eventually promoted to become the first female chief superintendent of the city's fire protection bureau.

She had her share of suitors during her early years at the fire department. There were always flowers on her office desk and baskets of fresh fruits from her admirers. But no one seemed to meet the standards that she had set for herself using Zeke's mould.

She knew it was unfair to her suitors, but she couldn't ignore the fact that her heart only yearned for Zeke. How she wished someone would come along, closely resembling Zeke. Or, someone who thought like Zeke. Or, talked like him. Or, at least told jokes like Zeke did. Could she simply wish for Zeke?

When Zeke entered the seminary, she felt like her heart had stopped beating. It was her first heartbreak without him having the faintest idea. She was quick to recover because his absence made it easy to forget.

Then, after a long while, a strange message popped up on her social media account. It was from someone named Zeke. She thought she had forgotten her feelings for him, but upon reading his message, she felt as if a spark was ignited deep inside her. Maybe the mind could forget but the heart always seemed to remember.

At first, Kit was suspicious. It was a strange message. He said he found her name on social media and was checking if she was the same Marikit Dimalanta he knew from school.

Given the proliferation of scammers and hackers, she had to be careful; she didn't want to fall victim. She wasn't the gullible type either. If this person was indeed Zeke Dipasupil, he'd better prove it.

> Zeke: Hi Kit! It's me, Zeke! Been away for so long. How are you?
> Kit: Why did the mute monkey fall in love with the other mute monkey?
> Zeke: I know. Because they have a mute-tual understanding.
> Kit: What do you call an ant that was born without a mouth?
> Zeke: A mute-ant.
> Kit was still thinking of another mute joke when Zeke messaged her.
> Zeke: Hey, it's me. You don't have to wreck your brain for another mute joke.

Kit couldn't describe how she felt knowing it was really Zeke who was messaging her. They agreed to meet at Conchita's that same night for dinner and went to a coffee shop for another round of catching up. Ever since, they had been meeting every Friday night.

'So, what happened at the office? How did you lose your job only to get it back again the next day?'

'It's a long story. You know Mr Z. He can be irrational and impulsive at times.'

'And you have a very bad temper.'

Zeke chuckled at the realization. 'Yeah, we're a really bad mix.'

'But you still respect the old man.'

'Yeah, he was like a father to me. Learnt a lot from him—what to do, what not.'

'And the fact that he couldn't imagine a day without you at the office.'

Zeke laughed, shaking his head. 'You really know how to feed my ego.'

Kit was smiling too. She liked making Zeke smile. For so long she had been staring at his eyes, particularly the area surrounding them, she observed how his laugh lines—or worry lines—had started to get more pronounced. She knew Zeke had been working long hours and getting less sleep. Their Friday night out was the only time she could meet him in person and ask about his work life. It was always about the office because he seldom talked about other things in his life. No matter how hard she wanted to be involved in the other parts of his life, she couldn't because she was just a friend, an outsider.

Thinking again, she wondered if opening up to Zeke about areas in her life other than work would prompt him to do the same. *No harm in trying*, she thought.

'Zeke, I'm just thinking … '

'Yep, what's up?' Zeke asked as he took a spoonful of sisig and washed it down with a sip of ginger ale. He had never liked the taste of beer.

'There's this guy I met at a conference, and he's sort of asking me out. But I'm still thinking if I should go or not.'

Kit was observing Zeke very closely. She liked the way he stopped midway through his drink, for a second or two, as if he was shocked to hear it.

'That's new. Tell me more about him,' he replied, trying to look unaffected.

A part of Kit wanted to make him feel jealous. But a part of her wanted an honest opinion of the guy.

She disclosed that the man's name is Police Sergeant Julian Archimedes Toribio, a Filipino-American forest ranger based in Atlanta, whom she'd met while attending an international fire and rescue conference at the Philippine International Convention Center (PICC).

During a 'getting-to-know' activity, the delegates were asked to go around and get at least five names. She was drawn to him because of the nickname pinned on his chest.

'Hello, Thor! Mr God of Thunder. So nice to meet you. How did you get the nickname if I may ask?'

'Hello, Kit! Good to meet you too.' He reached for her hand to shake it. 'Thor is short for my surname, Toribio,' he replied. 'How about your nickname? Is Kit short for Katherine?'

'You wouldn't be able to guess, so I'll just tell you. It's short for Marikit. It's a Filipino word meaning "beautiful". Not that I am but—'

Thor was quick to reply: 'But you are. I'm actually half-Filipino on my father side.'

If he hadn't revealed that he was half-Filipino, Kit wouldn't have guessed it because Thor stood at a towering six feet tall and had a Southern American accent. He worked as a forest ranger in Atlanta and was in Manila to attend the three-day conference. It was also a chance for him to visit his cousins and relatives whom he had not seen in years.

'So this guy called Thor is asking you out on a date,' Zeke said, as if seeking confirmation from Kit that he got the details right.

'I wouldn't really call it a date. Just a meet-up,' Kit replied defensively. She would rather not create an assumption this early because she barely knew the guy.

'So where do you plan to meet?' Zeke asked nonchalantly.

'I don't know … I'm not sure if I want to … Should I?'

It took Zeke a few seconds to answer. It wasn't an easy question. But he wouldn't want to limit her actions or hinder her from doing the things she wanted. It was her life, after all.

'I think you should go and give it a shot.'

'You really think so?' It was Kit's turn to seek confirmation.

'Yeah,' Zeke said rather half-heartedly, and his tone came across as indifferent. 'You wouldn't want to turn down the god of thunder, would you?'

Chapter Thirteen

Getting to the Bottom of Things

Sometimes the truth, like a glass of water, is all you need to calm down.
— Mrs Conchita Villafuerte

Mrs Conchita Villafuerte had her reservations about hiring a private investigator. While she was used to observing people, trying to read their character based on their facial expressions and bodily gestures, this time, she had a hunch that seemed so strongly connected to the very essence of her being. It kept her thinking and wondering for hours and hours, slowing her down, disrupting her daily routine and sometimes even making it hard for her to relax and sleep at night. Her maid Berta, noticed her unusual behaviour which was out of character.

'Is something bothering you, Ma'am?'

'I'm okay, thank you. Please get me a glass of water.'

Water always calmed her down. It eased her tension and helped her think more clearly.

Mrs Villafuerte had long wanted to find answers to the questions that popped in her head from the moment she had laid eyes on the young boy sitting in the waiting room of the cardiologist's clinic. He was sitting across from where she sat. He was reading what appeared to be a comic book, but when he lifted his head, she saw the face of her son, John Alexander, a student activist who had disappeared without a trace when

Martial Law was declared in the Philippines under Proclamation number 1081.

'Could he have sired a son?' She wanted so badly to know.

'Could this boy, by the grace of God, possibly be my grandson?'

After a little over a month of closely observing the boy from behind a fashion magazine, she finally decided to contact a private investigator. She couldn't sit still in the clinic's waiting area. Her eyes kept darting back to the boy sitting next to his mother.

Something inside her insisted that he was connected to her. She could be wrong, but she knew that she had to at least, act upon her intuition and try to find out the truth.

Mrs Villafuerte had been grieving for over a decade since her son failed to come home in 1972. During their last conversation, she remembered how his eyes gleamed with innocent excitement as he spoke about joining a group of students who freely expressed their views about changing the status quo, of letting the government know their sentiments. He had also signed up as a regular contributor to the campus newspaper that the university published twice a month.

'Mama, you should see how students are listening and letting their voices be heard. They are no longer bystanders because these issues affect everyone,' John Alexander exclaimed excitedly, like he was seeing a miracle unfolding right before his eyes.

She was proud of his achievements as a gifted public speaker and writer, joining inter-school debates and having published essays and poems in local dailies.

But he was headstrong, sometimes to a fault. On many occasions, he would give her a hundred reasons for why they should or should not proceed with a certain course of action.

Mrs Villafuerte couldn't forget that one time when he persuaded her into buying a car.

'Mama, I'm thinking of buying a car next year,' John Alexander mentioned casually.

'A car? Do you know how much a car costs?' his mother blurted out.

'Yes Mama. I know I don't have enough savings. Since buying a brand-new car isn't feasible at the moment, I'm okay with getting a second-hand car. A friend of a friend is selling their Volkswagen Beetle. The owner said I can pay in instalments.'

'And what would you do with it? I wouldn't want you picking up girls or driving drunk with your friends,' replied Mrs Villafuerte, expressing her fears openly.

'Mama, if we have a car, I'll save up gasoline money from my allowance. I'll also come home faster and safer from the dormitory every weekend. We can also drive to church on Sundays. Then we can have a picnic somewhere and drink your favourite sarsaparilla.'

Sarsaparilla was a popular soda drink in those days. Mrs Villafuerte smiled. Her son had created a very pleasant picture in her mind about what they could do with a car. She couldn't possibly argue after that.

John Alexander spoke with a certain level of passion and conviction that she seldom observed in other young men. And he always pointed out the good things not just for his own merit but also those that would benefit others. He was suave with a gift of persuasion. Her son's selfless nature and being openly truthful and outspoken were admirable. But being vocal about one's thoughts and convictions was also a dangerous thing during those times.

As a mother, she feared for his safety. She felt like he was joining the Katipunan, a secret society of revolutionists that had planned an insurrection against the Spaniards during the Spanish colonial era.

She would have supported him in whatever path he wanted to take, whatever career he intended to choose that would express his skills and interest—except, he chose to lend a voice to the weak and the powerless, to demand to be given what is due, to fight for a society that upholds justice and peace for all, no matter the cost.

She recalled how she had made him promise that he would come home that weekend to do three things: pick up his allowance, get fresh clothes (which she had ironed herself and thus, saved their helper from the trouble of getting nagged when the wrinkles weren't properly ironed out), and introduce the girl he intended to marry.

She wanted so much to meet the woman who had captivated her son's heart. She wanted to see her hands, if they were soft or rough, if she was willing to do house chores and keep a tidy house for the family that they intended to build. She wanted to see her hips, if they were big and round, capable of delivering children without difficulty. She wanted so much to have healthy grandchildren to dote on.

Superstitious in a way, she also wanted to check for moles or beauty marks, especially on her face. If they were near the temples, it could mean intelligence; if near the lips, it could be an indicator of loose lips; if under the eyes, which Mrs Villafuerte was very apprehensive of, it could mean the woman would soon be crying over her husband's death as a widow. That was definitely something Mrs Villafuerte wouldn't want to see.

But sadly, she never had a chance to meet the bride-to-be since John Alexander went missing. His teachers and classmates were also clueless about his whereabouts, wondering about his long unexcused absence from class. The college press office where he used to frequent as a contributing writer to the campus newspaper was closed down. The editors and newspaper adviser were unresponsive to her calls.

After her son's disappearance, Mrs Villafuerte had gone to the campus police station to file a missing person report. The police officers were accommodating but informed her that her son's case was one in more than seventy student disappearances they had on file.

'Are you sure your son did not run away?' they asked her.

'Is it possible that he got a girl pregnant and decided to raise a family on his own without your knowledge?' They continued to barrage her with questions that made her feel uncomfortable and queasy, like a headache was forthcoming. So she decided to walk away.

When she came back to follow up about the case two weeks later, the police assured her that they were working on it but when they took out the folder from the filing cabinet, it appeared unopened and dusty.

* * *

Special Investigator Rodolfo Blanco called just before lunchtime. He was hired six months prior by Mrs Villafuerte. Now it was time to reveal what he had discovered. He said he would come over to her house after lunch. The old lady was ecstatic. Six months was a long wait, but it was worth every peso spent.

Blanco's name was frequently referred to in social circles of the moneyed lot. He was considered the most sought-after private investigator. One woman found out that her husband had been cheating on her after Blanco provided her with a photograph of her husband smooching another woman inside his car. Another lady was able to confirm her suspicions that her husband had another family. But as it turned out, she wasn't the legal wife. Truth is, indeed, a double-edged sword.

Blanco had retired from his post in the NBI after serving the agency for forty-three years. He had been accepting small private investigating jobs to while away his time. He wasn't the type to keep still and just tend his garden at home. He wanted to wake up at the same time every day and follow the work routine that he had been engaging in for so long.

The job request from Mrs Villafuerte was simple: to confirm if her missing son was indeed dead and to identify if a boy who looked a lot like her son was her grandson.

She sat at the table at lunch but wasn't able to eat a morsel of food. The milkfish cooked in sour broth sent by the cook from the modest eatery that she had built was very appetizing. She could smell the delicious aroma of the long green chillies in the broth and see the fat in the fish belly almost bursting in the soup. But her anticipation was too much to bear; she couldn't stop her hands from trembling, and the anxiety was almost choking her.

The investigator walked into the living room of the old ancestral house with an air of confidence and sat on the sofa. He opened an innocuous-looking bag and produced a document. It was a copy of the birth certificate of a boy named Zechariah Dipasupil. Her son, who went missing during the Martial Law years, John Alexander Villafuerte, was listed in the box under 'Father's Name'.

'Ma'am, your son and his lady love initially planned to wed by the end of 1971 but wedding plans were postponed when he got deeply involved in campus activism. He wrote several articles in the campus newspaper that were regarded as subservient and anti-government. Unfortunately, circumstances led to his arrest and detention in an undisclosed location. He went missing thereafter, together with twelve other companions,' said Blanco as he read the findings of his investigation.

Mrs Villafuerte was listening intently while clutching a rosary to her chest. She let out a gasp upon hearing about her son's arrest and detention.

The investigator would pause every now and then to check on Mrs Villafuerte as he understood that his revelations could be too much for her to take.

'His lady love bore him a son in 1973 but since they weren't married, the boy carried his mother's name—Dipasupil. And yes, they were the mother and son that you met at the doctor's clinic.

Mrs Villafuerte received the copy of her grandson's birth certificate with tears of joy in her eyes.

'Zechariah … what a beautiful name!' The old lady exclaimed happily as her suspicions were confirmed. The boy in the waiting room of the doctor's clinic, who had an unmistakable resemblance to her son was, indeed, her own grandson.

Thereafter, Special Investigator Blanco paused for a while to carefully pick the right words: it was time to report the matter about his client's missing son.

As in the past, without intending to, he had uncovered more details than what his client had asked of him. Looking at Mrs Villafuerte, he felt that even though she looked strong and feisty on the outside, deep inside, she might have a weak heart. He wouldn't want to shock her with too many details. But he knew he had an obligation to disclose the facts that he had unwittingly discovered.

'About your missing son, Ma'am … I found evidence confirming that he was arrested by authorities along with many others for questioning … on charges relating to subversive acts and violent protests. He died a long time ago and was buried in an unmarked grave. I'm so sorry.'

Mrs Villafuerte couldn't stop the tears. She felt weak and nauseated. A house help rushed to offer a glass of water and a handkerchief.

'Where did they bury him? Can I go and visit his grave? Please tell me where to go. Please … ' she said in between sobs.

'He was buried along with the others … in a mass grave.'

Mrs Villafuerte was inconsolable. '*Ano'ng ginawa nila sa anak ko? Mananagot sila!* (What did they do to my son? They should be held accountable!)'

'The long arm of the law will make sure that the guilty will not go unpunished, and the victims will be given justice and their families indemnified for their loss,' was all he could say.

Mrs Villafuerte couldn't stop crying. Oh, how she missed her son John Alexander. She cried for her son, whose face she would never see again. She cried for his voice, his laughter, and his jokes that she would never hear. She cried for the warm hugs—he used to hug her every time he left the house—that she would never again feel against her skin. She cried for his unmade bed, his tossed-up cabinet, his muddy cross trainers, and all the mess that she would happily take if only she could see him again.

But John Alexander wasn't ever coming back. Could he have been tortured before he was killed? Could he have called her name before he died? She imagined the horrors that her son might have suffered. A mother could only take so much: she wailed like a woman experiencing the pains of childbirth, except she was mourning the death of her child, which was twice the pain and anguish.

Special Investigator Blanco could not stand the sight of a crying woman. It broke his heart to see her in such a pitiful state. It was the most difficult part of his job—revealing the truth that hurt another so deeply. He would do anything in his power to console her or at least lessen her grief.

After seeing a crucifix on the front door when he entered the house and the image of the Blessed Virgin Mary of Fatima venerated on an altar with fresh flowers, Special Investigator Blanco still had one last card to drop on the table—hopefully, one to console her.

'By the way, the *sepulturero* was kind enough to call on a priest to sprinkle holy water on the grave. Again, I'm so sorry to reveal these things but at least this will hopefully give you closure.'

Mrs Villafuerte was trying to compose herself. She smiled meekly and nodded behind the tears that refused to stop.

As he turned to leave, he handed her a piece of paper bearing an address and a phone number.

'Just a footnote, this is the address of your grandson and your supposed daughter-in-law. Sadly, she seemed unable to recover from the disappearance of your son as she is undergoing medication for a lot of ailments. You might want to give her a call before you visit.'

Chapter Fourteen

Of Memories and Ghosts

When ghosts from the past come back to haunt you, it only means two things: either you deal with them or spend your remaining days on the run.

—Bishop Pimentel

Special Investigator Blanco was a devout Catholic and kept a rosary made of luminous beads in his pocket as an expression of his devotion to the Blessed Virgin Mary. For him, the rosary was as powerful a weapon as his trusty mini revolver that he carried under his jacket.

One afternoon, after going on a pilgrimage to the Shrine of Our Lady of Antipolo and hearing mass in thanksgiving for all blessings received especially in light of his retirement, he went to the sacristy to see his old friend, Bishop Pimentel, who happened to officiate the mass that afternoon.

The kindly bishop was only too glad to see him and invited him inside the rectory to have some *merienda.* It was a happy reunion as the two men exchanged stories about the goings-on in their lives while biting into warm *pan de coco* and *ensaymada* and sipping on ice-cold soda bought from a nearby bakery. They talked about old times.

Special Investigator Blanco casually mentioned a missing person case that he was working on, not that he expected the bishop to help him.

'You're looking for a person who disappeared during the Martial Law years?' the bishop asked to confirm if he had heard it right.

'Yes. The young man disappeared just a few weeks before Martial Law was declared. His mother just wanted to confirm his death.'

The bishop was silent for a few moments, as if trying to recall an event in the past.

'A young newly-ordained priest approached me several years ago and asked if I could provide him some spiritual direction. He appeared troubled so I dropped what I was doing and gave him all my attention.

'The young priest was undecided if he should go back to his hometown or not. He was under some kind of pressure, so he thought that the fresh air and rural setting would help clear the cobwebs.

'I agreed with him on that point and advised that he took his leave as soon as possible.

'Before he left, he produced from under his arm a parcel wrapped in plastic. He said another man had asked him to take care of it. Apparently, he wasn't up to the task now that he had decided to go back to his hometown. So he asked if I could keep it until the time he gets back.

'It was a simple request of safekeeping so I assured him that the parcel would be safe in my care.

'A few weeks later, I was informed by the diocese that the young priest had died. Out of curiosity, I opened the parcel and found that it contained a logbook with a list of names. Still at a loss as to the value of the logbook, I prayed to God for guidance.

'Soon after, a man came to the rectory looking for me. He introduced himself as the owner of the logbook that the young priest had handed to me for safekeeping and said that he had lost contact with the young priest. The man was in his late sixties wearing an old but clean shirt. He had a tired and scared look on his face. He said that he was going back to his hometown and needed to take the logbook along with him.

'I told him that the priest also used the same alibi of going back home. And that the priest was dead.

'The man fell on his knees, asking for forgiveness for not telling the truth. He revealed that the logbook contained a list of people who were arrested or abducted and were executed thereafter. The man said he was given the ungodly task of burying the victims.

'The killers had told him that they would pay him to dig up graves and bury ghosts.

'"Ghosts? How could I possibly bury ghosts?" the man asked.

'"You better not look at them or they might haunt you in your sleep," the killers had said, snorting and sniggering like devils.

'The ghosts they were referring to were the people they had abducted and killed. They were all sorts—writers, teachers, university professors, reporters, lawyers, business people, human rights advocates, priests, nuns, government officials, and others who were tagged as radical thinkers and enemies of the administration. Even students were not spared.

'The first victim was a man with a bullet in his head who appeared to have been gagged to prevent him from talking or screaming. But since rigor mortis had set in, the man died with his mouth open wide.

'The second was a woman who appeared to have been gang-raped and then stabbed several times. Her scarlet uniform was soaked.

'The others that followed had bloodied faces and bore torture marks on their bodies. Some even had limbs or body parts missing.

'Taking pity on the victims, the man went to a friend who owned a textile shop and asked for factory rejects. He used the fabrics with defects to wrap the bodies before laying them in the mass grave.

'Thereafter, the man began having difficulty sleeping, claiming to have been visited by ghosts. Because of this, he decided to call on a newly-ordained priest, whom he knew as a boy from their neighbourhood and asked him to come and sprinkle holy water on the graves that he had dug. After that, the apparitions stopped, like they were released from the chains that bound them to the land of the living.

'After digging several burial grounds in a span of two weeks, the man couldn't take it any more. He summoned up all his courage to refuse the ungodly task by running away to hide but not before stealing the logbook containing the victims' names and entrusting it to his priest friend to keep it safe from the killers.

'Then, like a penitent seeking penance for his sins, the man disclosed the location of the mass graves that he had dug for the victims—in a hilly region on the outskirts of Manila.

'So there he was, standing before me, faced with the greatest dilemma of his life: whether he should claim the logbook and surrender it to the killers or keep it hidden and continue living on the run, always looking behind his shoulder.

'So I asked him, "Do you think they will let you live after giving the logbook back to them?"

'"No," he sadly replied. "I have witnessed too much."

'So I offered to keep the logbook until the storm "blew over".

'Before he left, the man asked to be prayed over. I told him to seek God's forgiveness and peace. After the pray-over, the man appeared to have been relieved of his burden. His face looked peaceful as he left the rectory. Such was the power of prayer.

'I don't know what has become of him because the man never returned.'

After recounting the incident, the bishop admitted that he had forgotten all about the logbook until now.

Scurrying to his room, the bishop got a bunch of keys, opened a small drawer inside his closet, took the parcel out and handed it to Special Investigator Blanco.

'By the grace of God, we have lived up to this moment to see the purpose of this book fulfilled before our eyes,' the holy man said.

Special Investigator Blanco had handled many homicide cases in the past, but none made him as jittery as this case. He saw his hands shaking as he unwrapped the parcel. It was, indeed, a logbook which, upon closer examination, seemed stained with dirt and what appeared to be dried blood.

The logbook could be full of fingerprints to bring the guilty to justice and grant peace to the families of those who had been screaming for it in their graves. But that would be a separate case.

Swiftly, he ran his fingers through the pages, reading each name on every line. He kept reminding himself that the list was not an ordinary list. It was written by evil men with evil hearts during a dark time.

As he turned pages upon pages of names, his fingers began to go numb.

These weren't names of people who died in an accident like a sunken ship's passenger manifest. These were people who should have been alive but were killed out of remorse and prejudice like the Jews killed by the Nazi during the Second World War.

Soon, he had mixed feelings as to whether or not he wanted to find the young man's name on the list. Finding his name would mean that the young man had died a horrible death in the hands of his tormentors. But it would also confirm his passing and give his mother the peace of mind that she had been denied for so long.

Then his eyes stopped upon seeing the name listed under entry number 1,081: John Alexander Villafuerte. He knew his mission was over.

Chapter Fifteen

Lost and Found

When people knock on your door, it is either because they want something from you or they got something for you. The former is always the case so I consider those who knock a big bother. But the old lady changed all that: not only did she rescue us from being lost, she also showed us the way home.

—Zechariah 'Zeke' Dipasupil

The young Zeke first heard the voice calling from outside their house. It was a Saturday, and he was relaxing at home watching his favourite cartoon TV series *Voltes V*. The voice sounded familiar, not impersonal like the salesmen selling vacuum cleaners or encyclopaedias. Zeke was used to answering the door, especially when his mother was resting in her room. She had been feeling unwell for the past couple of weeks and spent much of her time in bed.

When he peeped through the window, he was surprised to see the old lady from the doctor's clinic. She was smiling and asking about his mother and if it was a good time to see her. Oh, how the little boy's heart jumped with joy upon seeing her. He immediately went to his mother's room and declared, 'Mama! It's the lady from the doctor's clinic!'

'What? How?' His mother was too sleepy to fully realize what was going on.

Zeke excitedly ran to open the gate, his legs racing as fast as his heart. 'Good morning, please come in,' he said to Mrs Villafuerte like a gentleman and reached for her hand.

'*Mano po*. (Your hand please.)' He touched her hand to his forehead as a gesture of respect.

'God bless you,' whispered Mrs Villafuerte, proud to see her grandson's respectful behaviour.

'Oh, you look so grown up! Has it been a year already since I last saw you at the clinic? How are you? You look so handsome like your father … '

Zeke felt awkward at the mention of his father. How could this old lady know what his father looked like? Did she know him?

Seeing the boy up close, Mrs Villafuerte couldn't help but stare. She wanted to reach out and hold him because he was the nearest thing to holding her son, John Alexander, once again. But she decided to restrain herself for fear the boy might get an anxiety attack again. She followed him inside the house.

'My mother will see you shortly. Please have a seat,' Zeke said, while bowing respectfully before disappearing into the kitchen.

As Mrs Villafuerte sat waiting on the faded blue sofa that had seen better days, the old lady's eyes wandered around. She couldn't help but scrutinize the cramped living room, shabby curtains and cheap furniture. There were broken tile floors that had been put together like a puzzle. The ceiling had leak stains and the walls needed a paint job.

If this meeting had happened in 1971, the time when she badly wanted to meet the woman that her son so wanted to marry, her lips would have curled in disdain and her eyebrows would have raised in disapproval, but she was glad it didn't.

Slightly snobbish and condescending, Mrs Villafuerte was not one to be easily pleased. First impressions were important to her. But now, she didn't feel like passing judgement. She must have left her old self by the door. Instead, she only felt warmth, love and acceptance deep inside her. The years must have mellowed her.

Looking at the living room in a different light, what she saw was a house that may have been lacking in space but was otherwise orderly and clean. The furniture brought at a discount or from a surplus shop could be a reflection of the owner's prudent use of money. Extravagance was thrown out the window.

The roof and walls, since she wasn't privy to the owner's plans, may have long been scheduled for repairs and repaint. She shouldn't be too quick to judge.

But she couldn't ignore the fact that the house had a drab look about it. There was an air of loneliness, save for the noise coming from the boy's television. A kind of languor that weighs down on occupants, snuffing out anything bright or happy.

To anyone quick to pass judgement, the house might not have appeared as an ideal place to raise a child. But the mother and child who lived here weren't strangers any more. They were the family of her son and, therefore, hers too.

Shortly, she heard footsteps coming from the kitchen. It was Zeke carrying a glass of orange juice and a small pack of crackers. He was smiling but in an embarrassed kind of way.

'Mama is just dressing up. She isn't used to receiving visitors. But I'm so glad you came … I got you some snacks. It's not really much since we haven't gone to the grocery yet … sorry the juice isn't cold. We ran out of ice.'

The old lady smiled kindly at the young boy.

'You shouldn't have bothered,' she said in a motherly way. 'But I wouldn't say no to the orange juice. I like fruit juices better than soda.'

Mrs Villafuerte was only too glad to see a smile form on the young boy's lips. Seeing how she took the glass of juice from the tray, he didn't look embarrassed any more.

She drank the juice. It wasn't cold as she would have preferred it, but since it was prepared by her grandson, it tasted just as good.

Stepping out of her room, Zeke's mother was delighted to meet the old lady; her face had an instant glow. She seemed to have forgotten her pain and her sadness. Even her vertigo seemed to have faded away. She didn't feel weak either.

They talked for hours like good friends who were happy to see each other after a long time.

During this time, Zeke minded his own business in a corner, watching cartoons on TV. But he was silently observing his mother from his peripheral view. He had never seen her looking so alive. He was only too glad to see her talk, smile and laugh again. It was as if she had found her old cheerful self from a long time ago.

'I think it is time for me to reveal why I came to visit,' the old lady said. She reached into her bag and brought out an old photograph of a man.

When Zeke's mother recognized the man in the photograph, she was aghast and couldn't believe her eyes. The man in the photograph was John Alexander, the father of her son, the man whom they both loved and lost. She couldn't control her emotions as tears began to flow ceaselessly, having been held at bay for so long.

Seeing his mother cry, Zeke immediately rushed to her side to see what the matter was. And there, he saw the photograph she lovingly held in her hands.

'Is he … my father?' Zeke managed to asked, his voice cracking. It was the question he had long been wanting to ask.

His mother nodded in between sobs.

Zeke looked and marvelled at how closely he resembled the man in the photograph. They had the same soulful eyes, the same thin lips, the same bushy eyebrows, although his father's nose seemed more high-bridged than his.

The photograph felt strange in his hand. It was as if he was staring at his older self in the mirror. And the reflection seemed to be smiling back at him, like the man was happy to see him too.

Zeke felt his eyes sting.

'Papa … papa … papa …,' Zeke uttered the words for the first time. And he felt good, like he had suddenly found the missing piece of the biggest puzzle in his life.

'Call it a woman's intuition or something else, but I knew right away that you might be my long-lost grandson when I saw you at the doctor's clinic,' the old lady said. 'So I hired a private investigator who later confirmed my suspicions.'

The old lady held Zeke and his mother in a tight embrace. They were once lost and alone. Now they were found.

The details of how John Alexander died were not easy to disclose. But Mrs Villafuerte did not baulk, because it would be unfair to mask the truth that had been kept under wraps for so long.

'John Alexander died at the hands of evil men. The private investigator that I hired was able to confirm that he, along with twelve of his companions, were among the Martial Law victims. And only God knows what kind of suffering he underwent before he died. He was buried along with the others in a mass grave.'

Unlike the old lady who cried and wailed upon hearing how John Alexander suffered, Zeke's mother wept only silent tears. They were tears of sorrow, regret, gratitude and relief.

Deep inside, she felt proud because the man she so loved had bravely stood up against the ruling powers and, together with the others, raised his voice against oppression, violence and injustice. With the dictator abdicating his throne in a bloodless revolution, she knew that John Alexander did not die in vain. His sacrifice along with others' would be forever remembered.

Still, she couldn't stop the tears from flowing. She had waited for so long, hoping he might show up at her doorstep one day.

But now her fears were confirmed. And the waiting had finally come to an end. After she was able to compose herself, she revealed to the old lady that after giving birth to Zeke, she had abandoned the idea of ever seeing her parents again out of shame since she had given birth out of wedlock.

'It is not good for you to live by yourself, disconnected from people who love you. It is also not good for the boy. He has a right to know his kin, that he belongs to a family,' said Mrs Villafuerte in a calm but firm voice. She felt that she must talk sense into Zeke's mother, who had long been enslaved by her depression.

Zeke's mother hung her head. Admittedly, she had not been thinking straight. The loneliness and the depression had made her shun the world and build a wall around herself and Zeke.

'Don't you want to see your family again?' Mrs Villafuerte asked in a motherly tone.

'God knows how I yearned to see them,' replied Zeke's mother. 'I'm just not sure if they will accept Zeke. But I also don't want him to grow without meeting his lolo and lola.'

The old lady smiled. 'When do you plan to visit them? I think I should come along and introduce myself as their *balaeng hilaw*,' she chuckled.

Upon hearing those words, Zeke saw his mother flash a smile from behind her tears. It was a different kind of smile this time, not the empty one he was used to seeing.

She embraced the old lady once more because she no longer felt alone. The old lady's presence made her feel that everything would be all right, just like John Alexander did.

Chapter Sixteen

The Long Trip Home

Home can be a lot of things. It can mean a structure, a person, or a particular moment that makes you feel loved and peaceful inside.

—Zeke's mother

Ever since the day of the old lady's visit, subsequent events transpired in quick flashes, like the shuffling of a deck of cards or flipping of pages in a book. Zeke wanted to hold on to the rolling scenarios. He wanted to make them last at least a bit longer. But they were like leaves swiftly blown away by the monsoon winds, like sand slipping through his fingers.

The trip to his mother's hometown in Lipa City in Batangas province would be an adventure for any teenager, but for Zeke, who had never left the city, it was more so. It was like discovering another village on the other side of the mountain; rather, two mountains—Mount Makulot and Mount Malarayat. Lipa City was in a valley between these two mountains.

Zeke had never felt as comfortable sitting on the cushioned seats of the large and spacious van that Mrs Villafuerte—or 'Mamita' as she preferred to be called—had hired for the trip.

Mamita had given him the privilege of sitting in the front passenger seat beside the driver, so he could have a full view of the road. After all, it was Zeke's first out-of-town trip so she wanted to make it memorable for him.

Mamita's personal assistant, Berta, brought along two ice chests filled with snacks and drinks. There were bread and pastries, too, to satiate any hunger pangs during the trip. But Zeke was too excited to eat. In fact, he didn't feel hungry at all. He had brought along his camera and stuffed an overnight bag with extra clothes, just in case he needed to change.

The group left Manila as early as seven o'clock in the morning. Halfway through the trip, Zeke felt nauseous. He fumbled through his pockets for some hard candies but all he had were empty wrappers. Turns out, he had been absent-mindedly popping candies into his mouth the whole time on the road!

For Zeke, this was the longest road trip ever. Though he threw up twice—they had to find a grassy spot on the roadside where they could stop and rest—he didn't mind. He was smiling throughout the entire ordeal.

'Don't worry about me. I'm absolutely fine,' he declared, wiping his mouth with the wet tissue Berta had handed him.

His mother whispered to Mrs Villafuerte, 'He's never been on the road this long. But he'll get used to it. He's a fighter.'

'I'm sure he will,' Mrs Villafuerte mused. 'I think it's the excitement that is making his stomach flip.'

The view of the mountains getting larger and more majestic as they approached them on the expressway and the road getting narrower and dustier as they went past the poblacion going to his grandparents' house in Barangay Pangao would remain etched in his mind forever.

For Zeke, meeting his Lolo Artemio and Lola Petra for the first time was a magical moment. But watching his mother run into the outstretched arms of her ageing parents was even more magical. The smile on his mother's face was indescribable. Her laughter sounded like the innocent shrieks of a young girl. Her ailments didn't manifest any symptoms at all. She was a picture of good health, exhilaration and bliss, as if being home and seeing her family had cured all her pains.

Meanwhile, Zeke's lolo and lola were proud to see him all grown up. They embraced and kissed him on the head but not without a sniff; they would want to remember the moment along with the scent of his hair. They had missed a lot during his growing-up years.

They showed him around the farm, where they raised chickens for eggs and pigs for meat. A bee farm was the latest addition, given the growing demand for pure honey amid the proliferation of artificial ones in the market.

Aside from livestock, they also grew Barako coffee and black pepper.

Zeke caught a whiff of the harvested black pepper that was dried and stored inside a storage room at the back of the house. He ended up snorting and sneezing. His allergic rhinitis was acting up again. The maid Berta was quick to hand him a tissue.

'Thank you, Ate,' said Zeke. 'Don't worry, I'm okay.' He didn't want his grandparents to worry about him.

His grandparents also grew fruit-bearing trees like lanzones, rambutan, papaya, bananas and dalandan. As food producers, they were proud to contribute to the food supply in their community.

Since the weather was humid, lunch was served on a large table made of bamboo, which was brought outside the house and placed under the shade of a large mango tree.

They feasted on *sinaing na tulingan*, a popular comfort food from Batangas. They ate it on banana leaves with boiled white rice and slices of tomatoes and green mango with *bagoong* on the side.

They also enjoyed fresh *buco* juice, which came from freshly harvested coconuts pried open using a *bolo*. In the afternoon, they snacked on *suman* dipped in sugar and overflowing *barako* coffee, whose beans were traditionally ground, boiled in water, and flavoured with brown sugar.

'*Pumarine kayo kahit linggo-linggo at tayo'y kakain ng ganire. Nagpapitas na rin ako ng mga prutas para maiuwi ninyo.* (You can visit us every week and we'll eat together like this. We also harvested some fruits you can take home with you),' Zeke's grandfather Artemio said. He was proud of the abundant produce of his farm.

Zeke sheepishly smiled when he was introduced to his cousins. He felt awkward since it was his first time meeting them. His cousins also felt the same way. Zeke was sitting on the sofa with them, but he didn't know what to say. Then he had an idea.

'Hey, do you also watch *Voltes V*?' he asked.

'Yes, we do,' his cousins exclaimed in unison. 'It's our favourite show on TV!'

Soon they were talking and laughing and exchanging stories about this well-loved cartoon franchise from Japan that was popular in the mid-1980s.

Towards the evening, when it was time to go home, his grandparents made sure their van was filled to capacity with all kinds of wonderful things to take home, including two live chickens in a native *bayong* punched with holes, coffee beans, ground black pepper, and a wide variety of fruits in season.

Mamita was so moved by their generosity that she promised to come back sometime soon and cook for them her speciality, pork sisig and *paella valenciana*.

But of them all, it was Zeke's mother who was the happiest. She laughed and cried since she never thought that a day would come when she would be reunited with her family again. It was a dream come true.

The scent and sounds of the farm animals, the aromatic barako coffee, the savoury home-cooked meals, the smile on her parent's faces as they saw them entering the gate, all created a beautiful memory that she would cherish forever.

But her happiness was short-lived. No one expected her happiness to make a sudden downturn. A week after the trip, her CT scan and MRI results came back positive. Her doctor confirmed that her frequent episodes of fatigue, vertigo and weight loss were symptoms of a deeper illness.

In six weeks' time, the family came together again, but this time at the hospital. Zeke's mother did not want to continue her treatment and instead wanted to spend her remaining days with her family at home.

Zeke was inconsolable. His mother may had given up, but he didn't want to. To his young mind, it felt that there had to be something else he could do to save his mother's life.

One night, as Zeke lay on a cot by his mother's bedside, he thought of God. He thought about the words he heard in Chapel Hill. So he prayed: 'God, can you hear me? You know that my mother is all that I have in the world. Please don't take her away from me. I don't know what to do without her.'

Then he heard a voice. It was the same gentle voice. Was he imagining things again? No. He doubted it coming from his mind. But he heard it in his heart.

'She'll always be with you as I am too.'

In her last will, Zeke's mother wanted her son to be under the care of Mamita, explicitly requesting her help in telling Zeke all he needed to know about his father, John Alexander. It was something she had admittedly failed to do. She said she had allowed grief and regret, longing and waiting, anger and hate to get the better of her. And while doing so, she had unmindfully pushed into oblivion the beautiful and vivid memories she had of John Alexander. Now, no matter how hard she tried, everything about him seemed clouded and grey, like under a filter of sorts. She couldn't recall anything happy, fun or pleasant when she thought of him. Because of this, she knew that it wouldn't be fair to Zeke if she answered his questions with faint, sad memories of John Alexander.

When the old lady and new family members came into their lives, Zeke's world had changed. All of a sudden, their small patch of land where their house stood no longer seemed small. It became bigger, brighter and livelier than ever before. The boundaries had been shattered. Every now and then, he would shuttle from their house in Manila to Mamita's palatial house in Quezon City. And on most weekends, he would visit his grandparents on their farm in Lipa City.

But just as quickly as the new had come, the old was gone.

The wake and the funeral happened so fast that Zeke couldn't quite make sense of what was happening. Suddenly, he felt alone. He shied away from people and was silent most of the time, unwilling to talk.

His young heart was heavy with anger. He was asking God—why.

God, are you there? My mother is a good person. Why did you take her away from me? What had she done to deserve to die? And now I'm alone. Yes, I have Mamita and my Lolo and Lola and my cousins. But I have just met them. They don't know who I am deep inside. They won't understand me. I want my Mama. I want to go home.

Then Zeke heard the voice say: 'Your mother is home. And you are home too.'

After the funeral, Mamita welcomed Zeke into her home, a large two-storey house from the 1950s, when the country was experiencing growth and expansion after the war. The house had undergone a number of repairs and renovations, including fixing damaged floors and roofs caused by typhoons. And more recently, cracked walls and floors due to earthquakes. But the house withstood the test of time and had been frequently featured in magazines as an architectural beauty reflecting the growth and prosperity of its time.

Widowed at a young age, Mamita had lived with her only son John Alexander. After her son went missing, the house felt empty as she only had the servant girl Berta to keep her company.

When Zeke moved in, Mamita gave him the option of picking his room since there were three vacant ones on the upper floor. The first room had grey walls; it was large and spacious with mid-sized windows. The second was a yellow room. Although a bit smaller than the first room, it had larger windows. The third was white, average-sized, with two windows situated across each other. He could see the sun rise and set from the two windows in the room—one facing the east, the other facing the west.

Zeke never had his own room since their house was small, and he shared the single bedroom with his mother. Now everything was changing. He was to pick a room that he could call his own, design it according to his liking, and arrange his things the way he wanted to. A carpenter would be summoned to make the adjustments.

He was so used to depending on his mother's good judgement for everything in his life. Now it was time to make his own choices.

Zeke went inside each of the rooms. He considered the size and layout of the furnishings, how he would utilize the space and how his things would fit in them. After closely examining the colours and how each room made him feel, he decided to pick the white room.

Mamita was secretly pleased because the white room once belonged to her beloved son, John Alexander. She had never used the room since, after putting away all his things in the attic. Now her grandson had chosen the revered room as his own, as if claiming it as his father's legacy.

Before telling Zeke, Mamita asked him what made him choose the white room.

'I'm not sure, Mamita. I just liked it the moment I entered it. It feels like home.'

Chapter Seventeen

An Eyewitness Account

When pride cannot accept the painful truth, it tags it as a lie and looks for ways to mask it.

—Yumi Salvacion

That same afternoon when the story of the dead boy appeared on the front page of *The Manila Daily Star*, the phone lines in the newsroom had been burning with calls and enquiries from TV news programmes, talk shows, non-government organizations, human rights groups, and others.

Even Mr Zultan's office wasn't spared. His secretary, Des, had been receiving calls one after the other. The efficient young woman would promptly write down the caller's name, contact numbers, and the nature of enquiry.

Zeke had been inside Mr Zultan's office for over an hour now. Des had already served a second pot of coffee and felt another one might soon be due. They were discussing, or more appropriately, debating over the next steps to take since the article seemed to have stirred a hornet's nest.

They reviewed a long list of people seeking appointments for an interview. They definitely needed a follow-up story. Zeke already had the boy's address as well as the contact details of the policemen involved. He wanted to take on the task of writing the follow-up story, since he had a background in investigative journalism. But Zultan would hear none of it.

'I was talking to the junior reporter who wrote the story. He said can't do it,' said Zeke in a matter-of-fact way.

'Why can't he?' Zultan asked, trying to mask something he already knew.

'Apparently, he's indisposed because he returned to his hometown to be with his family. He said he might take the entire week off. We cannot wait that long.'

'I agree. I can assign it to another field reporter.'

'Why assign it to others when you already have a volunteer right in front of you?' Zeke flashed the sweetest smile he could muster.

Zultan scoffed in annoyance. He took a sip of coffee and nibbled on a cookie that was served on a tray by his secretary.

'Do you know what I hate the most, Mr Dipasupil?'

'No, Sir,' Zeke replied respectfully.

'I hate to see great minds and raw talent get wasted because of impudence and reckless disobedience.'

It was Zeke's turn to be silent. He couldn't quite find the appropriate response.

'Do you want to know the real deal?' Zultan asked. 'That junior reporter is not on a leisure trip with his family … He's in his hometown trying to lie low because he has been receiving death threats since that story came out.'

Zeke was dumbfounded. He hadn't realized the gravity of the situation up until then. He paused, letting the information sink in, before saying, 'I'm sorry. I wasn't aware.'

'So now you know that this isn't something to toy around or do on a whim. I'll assign the story to another reporter who I know can handle the pressure.'

But Zeke was unfazed. He was not about to give up. 'Sir, with all due respect, I wouldn't insist if I couldn't handle it! Please let me write the follow-up story.'

The pressure was mounting. Zultan was losing his patience.

'It's not your damn job! Do I have to repeat your job description to remind you what your responsibilities are? I don't want another shouting match with you. I've already made my decision.'

Zeke knew when to insist and when to stop. He knew it was futile to argue further so he took his journal and pen, and walked out the door. Before the door completely closed, Zultan caught Zeke talking to Des, complimenting her for the coffee.

'The coffee was superb! Thanks, Des!'

'I made it just the way you like it, Zeke!'

Zultan smiled to himself. He had always admired Zeke. He liked his work ethics, the way he related to others, his attitude and especially his character. He was down-to-earth and always talked to people regardless of their stature. He was extremely generous with his compliments, a sign of a heart that is sincere and grateful.

Zultan felt like Zeke was the son he never had. He wouldn't want to put him in harm's way. He had seen many good journalists get threatened, abducted, tortured, and killed. He had lost colleagues and good friends. He wouldn't dare risk Zeke. He wouldn't want to lose a man with a good heart.

* * *

Back in his office, Zeke was feeling down. Who wouldn't? He knew he had the power of reasoning and persuasion. He knew he had always got his way. But today was not his day. Still, his mind bothered. He was still trying to think of a good reason to do it.

'Should I write the follow-up article or not? Should I go against Mr Zultan's wishes or not? Please God, give me a sign,' he found himself praying.

Suddenly his phone rang. It was Kit. She was asking if he could pick up her cat, Stella, from the grooming salon since her car had broken down and had to be brought to a repair shop. It would take some time to get the repairs done.

Zeke obliged.

The Good Groomer's pet salon was located about twelve kilometres from Zeke's office. But he didn't mind the drive. He felt like he needed a break, a reason to get out of the office, take the road, and rethink his options.

Driving, like smoking, helped him think and analyse things from a different perspective. It could be the act of getting out of the place, stepping away from all the action and re-looking at the entire picture from a new angle.

Zeke never really liked cats because they reminded him of the annoying cats he used to see in the bay walk area when he was young. The stray cats roamed freely like they owned the place. They were noisy, always meowing like they had the right to complain, and followed him for scraps.

But Stella was different. She was a white Himalayan with large, blue expressive eyes. Her meows were soft and sounded like a chime. Zeke also liked the fact that Stella preferred quiet environments, very much like him.

At the grooming salon, he walked up to the receptionist and enquired about Stella.

'I'll get Stella for you,' the kind attendant said with a smile. She returned with the cat inside a pink pet carrier.

Zeke paid the grooming fee and received the carrier from the attendant.

'You must be Mr Dimalanta? Here's your cat,' she said, mistaking him for Kit's husband.

'Oh no. I'm just a friend,' Zeke protested but the attendant failed to hear his voice and was already handling another customer.

Zeke walked to his car, put the pet carrier on the front seat, and seemed to be in a mood to talk with animals.

'Hey Stella, the attendant mistook me for your owner's husband. What can you say about that?'

'That's preposterous!' Zeke replied to himself, in a cat-like voice. He was putting words in Stella's mouth.

'I thought so too. But what if, just what if, we ended up together?'

'I wouldn't bet on that. Kit doesn't like you, one tiny bit.'

'Okay, how about if I buy you some canned fish? Do you think you can help change her mind?'

'Hmm. That can be arranged.'

'Good cat!' Zeke smiled to himself. The mounting pressure at work must be making him delusional.

As he turned the key to start his car's engine, he noticed the receipt taped on the side of Stella's carrier. The receipt contained the brand name of the grooming salon, its contact number, and address.

Suddenly, the address seemed familiar. Zeke remembered the address of the dead boy. It was in the same area.

Zeke felt his heart thumping in his chest. Was this the sign he had been asking for?

Something inside him was telling him to drive away and deliver Stella to Kit, because it was the reason he was there in the first place. But another voice was telling him to go and look for the boy's house. It seemed fate had placed him on that very spot for a purpose. His presence at that very moment inside the grooming salon on a narrow street paved with asphalt where electric wires hung loosely overhead and people came and went with their pets unmindful of the cramped space and the shabby neighbourhood was not circumstantial: it was providential.

Quickly, he drove off, looking for the location of the boy's house. At this time, there would be a lot of people attending the boy's wake. He was thankful that he didn't have any business meetings in the office, so he was dressed in a regular polo shirt and jeans that day. He wouldn't want to draw undue attention wearing a business attire.

Zeke faced no trouble asking for directions from bystanders smoking outside a barbershop. Soon, he was able to reach the boy's address.

As expected, there were a lot of people attending the wake. The boy's apartment was located within a row of apartments inside a compound. The gate of the compound was flung open to welcome those who had come to mourn with the family.

The boy's casket was infused with light from several lamps that were set up by the funeral parlour. It was painted white with gold cherubims exuding peace and innocence. Fragrant *sampaguita* flowers dotted the edges of the half-open casket. Surrounding the casket were funeral wreaths from the mayor's office, the congressman's office, and the barangay chairman's office, all signifying their condolences for the unexpected demise of someone so young. The flowers, mostly lilies and anthuriums, were pale yet beautifully arranged. A smiling photo of the boy was displayed on top of his casket.

Some old women were reciting prayers for the dead in a corner. Another woman was praying the rosary. There were children milling around the snack table collecting candies and cookies.

Youthful chatter could be heard from a group of teenagers dressed in school uniform, probably his classmates. They were too young to be mourning for someone their age. Some shed silent tears while others couldn't help but crack jokes to lighten the sombre mood.

'*Huwag nga kayong maingay dyan, baka maingayan si Jun-Jun at biglang bumangon.*' (Please keep quiet or Jun might suddenly rise up because of the noise.)

On a chair nearest to the coffin sat a middle-aged woman, probably the boy's mother. Zeke approached the woman and introduced himself.

'They killed my son,' the woman said amid bitter emotions flowing from her eyes. 'Are you a reporter?'

'Yes I am. But I'm not here to write a story. I'm here to extend my condolences. I'm so sorry for your loss.'

The woman couldn't quite contain her emotions.

'Do you know the pain of losing two people you love just in a span of six months? I've been working as an OFW abroad for more than ten years. I came home last April because my husband was killed in an accident at the construction site. His co-workers said he was accidentally electrocuted. But I doubted that. I knew my husband better than they did. I knew that somebody killed him. But for reasons I don't know.

'And now, my son is dead. He was shot by policemen who said he was a drug runner trying to escape. But my son is innocent! He is not a drug runner as reported in the news! Why don't you media people find out the truth before you make a report?' said the woman whose hands were trembling with grief and anger.

Zeke could feel the rising emotions of the mother. He wanted to bring a little consolation, if not justice, to the boy's grieving family by finding out what really happened. But seeing how distraught she was, he deemed it best to give the family time to grieve.

'I want to help in any way I can. I'm here to know the truth. Again, I'm so sorry for your loss,' he said.

'My son is innocent! You are killing my son again and again by telling lies! I want justice for my son!' The woman broke into sobs. Other women at the wake came by her side to console her.

As Zeke turned to leave, a young girl crossed his path. She wasn't looking at him as she walked past, but what she said puzzled him.

'*May nakita ako.* (I saw something.)' It was unmistakable that her words were meant for him to hear.

The girl appeared to be older than the dead boy, probably in her early twenties. She was wearing a cap over long curly hair, which she had tied neatly in a braid. An oversized shirt hid her figure, but skinny jeans and off-white sneakers showed off her shapely legs.

He tried to catch up with the girl as she walked out into the street. But she didn't seem to notice him—or pretended not to—as she showed no sign of slowing down.

She walked a few more blocks then turned a corner and entered a twenty-four-hour convenience store. He followed her inside the store.

'Why have you come to the wake? Are you a reporter?' she asked when he finally caught up with her.

'Yes, I am,' Zeke said as he showed her his press ID. He knew he shouldn't be meddling with the dead boy's case as agreed with Mr Zultan. But he couldn't just let this opportunity to know the truth pass. Otherwise it would be an injustice.

'Do you know anything about what happened?'

The young girl looked hesitant. She looked around the store. There were a number of people buying food and some lining at the counter.

'We can find another place if you don't feel safe here,' Zeke offered.

The young girl looked scared but was willing to talk about what she saw that night. She seemed to be carrying a heavy load and was looking for someone to tell to unburden herself.

Zeke invited the young girl to a coffee shop. He ordered two lattes. They found an unoccupied table at the farthest corner near the washroom.

Zeke positioned himself facing the entrance so he could easily see the people entering the shop. The girl sat with her back turned—it was best not to expose her face to the crowd.

After a short introduction, the girl named Yumi, started her narrative.

'We call him Jun-Jun, short for Eliseo Junior, since he carried his father's name. I've known him since we were young. He was the eldest in a brood of three. His father worked as an electrician in a construction company while his mother worked as a domestic helper abroad. His family used to occupy the smallest apartment unit next to ours.

'When his mother left to work abroad, their lives improved a bit. At first I felt envious because they were able to move to the biggest unit, the one originally occupied by the owner. But even if they had a bit more money to spend, Jun-Jun remained down-to-earth. He was a good friend—funny, smart and talented. He was a scholar at the city's Science High School. He wanted to take up culinary in college but he never got the chance to tell his parents … about what he wanted … and … about his real self.'

The girl's voice began to crack as she recounted the details of what she saw that night.

'I came home late that night because my shift at a fast food store ends at midnight. Since I missed the last trip of the tricycle going to our house, I had no choice but to walk all the way from the jeepney terminal.

'It was dark. As I approached noiselessly on foot, I saw at a distance three men and a boy. I quickly hid behind a lamp post overshadowed by an old Sampaloc tree.

'I recognized the boy as Jun-Jun, and the three men were policemen in uniforms. Two of the men were brandishing their guns as they kept asking Jun-Jun something about drugs. The third policeman who appeared to be the youngest among the three just kept watch.

'Jun-Jun was crying, saying he didn't know anything about what they were saying. But I know he was crying because he was also afraid of the guns that they were carrying.

'Jun-Jun never liked guns. Ever since we were young, he preferred dolls and cooking pots. But he never told his parents about it. He was afraid they wouldn't accept him.

'The policemen were barraging him with questions, trying to make him confess. When they could not get Jun-Jun to confess to anything, they became angry.

'Jun-Jun was kneeling, pleading and begging them to let him go home. He said he had to prepare for a test the next day.

'But the men showed him no mercy. One of them told Jun-Jun to run. And he did. Then the fat policeman began to shoot at him.

'The young rookie tried to intervene, pointing his gun at the shooter, asking him to stop shooting. But Jun-Jun had already been hit. The rookie ran to him and gave him first aid while the more senior police officer called an ambulance.

'Soon, Jun-Jun's relatives and neighbours arrived at the scene. Perhaps they were alarmed because they heard the gunshots.

'Then an ambulance arrived and took Jun-Jun to the hospital. But I heard he didn't last the night.'

As tears ran down her eyes, Yumi wiped them away with her hand. 'He begged them to let him go. I know they got the wrong guy. He was an innocent school boy worrying about his test the next day but they shot him just the same. Why did they have to kill an innocent and helpless boy?'

Seeing the young girl crying over the death of her friend, Zeke also found himself teary-eyed. For the first time in his life, Zeke couldn't stop his eyes from welling up. He wept for the death of a stranger, a boy he never knew, an innocent youngster caught in the middle of a war against illegal drugs.

The boy had pleaded for his life, a life that held so much promise. But his cries had fallen on deaf ears that refused to acknowledge the truth. And because of the evil that hates the truth, the self-consuming pride that puts the blame on others, his voice had been silenced.

But not for long. Zeke knew there was a reason he was sent on an errand and why he had found himself in the boy's neighbourhood. Coincidences happen for a purpose. He would lend a voice to the voiceless and shine a light on the truth about Jun-Jun's death.

After the conversation ended, Zeke asked Yumi what she wanted in return for the information she provided. The young girl's only request was for Jun-Jun's story to be told to the world as she had witnessed it, because people needed to know what had really happened that night.

And Zeke, as the hard-hitting and faithful truth-seeker that he was, vowed to honour Jun-Jun's death with a detailed revelation of the truth.

He walked back with Yumi to the boy's wake and tried to talk to the boy's relatives, who might have witnessed the incident to corroborate Yumi's statement.

The boy's uncle Mang Edgar who also lived in the same compound gave an account of what he remembered of the incident.

'After my brother Eliseo died a few months ago from an accident at the construction site where he worked, I acted as a guardian to Jun-Jun and his siblings, since their mother works abroad. I would check on them in the morning before going to work and in the evening, I would see them and ask how their day went.

'Jun-Jun, being the eldest, was very responsible. He would wake up early, cook their meals and help his siblings prepare for school. He was a very good cook. I remember asking him to cook *kaldereta* or *menudo* on special occasions.

'Anyway, when the three policemen entered our compound that night, I was both surprised and worried. They introduced themselves as police operatives of Oplan Tokhang, and they were looking for my brother, Eliseo Reyes. I told them that perhaps they were mistaken because my late brother was a good man. They didn't believe me when I told them that he was dead. They wouldn't take my word for it. They thought we were hiding him.

'The police were rude. One of the policemen even appeared to be drunk. They asked everyone in the compound to line up outside their apartment and declare their names aloud.

'When Jun-Jun declared that his name was Eliseo Reyes Jr, one of the policemen immediately took hold of him, saying his name was on their drug list. But I protested, saying they were mistaken. Jun-Jun was just a child. He was only fourteen. They must have mistaken him for his father because they have the same name. But they wouldn't listen. They were keen on making an arrest right then and there.

'They took Jun-Jun but I ran after them. Then one of the policemen pointed his gun at me saying they will just ask him questions. They threatened me saying I could get hurt if I hindered them from fulfilling their duty. I knew something bad was going to happen to Jun-Jun and even then I couldn't help him.'

Mang Edgar began to cry recalling his helplessness at the situation. He cried because even though he called for help, it was too late.

'I called on the barangay captain for help. He arrived along with four community patrollers, barangay *tanod*. But shortly after, we heard gunshots fired one after the other. We rushed towards the direction of the shots and saw Jun-Jun on the ground, wounded. His leg was bleeding. The youngest of the three policemen was trying to give him first aid to stop the bleeding in his leg.

'We were told by the senior officer that it was an accidental shooting and assured me that they would take care of his hospital expenses.

'When the ambulance arrived, the medical team discovered that Jun-Jun had been shot elsewhere too, and he had lost a lot of blood. They were able to take him to the emergency room but he died soon after.

'The autopsy showed that he was first hit in the leg from behind. Then, he was hit in the groin, maybe when he turned around. Those heartless criminals killed my nephew, and now they want to make it look like a damn accident! Who are they fooling?'

Chapter Eighteen

Stop the Story

Intimidation only becomes real if you let it. Otherwise, it's just a twelve-letter word with 'timid' in between.

—Benjamin Zultan

It was a Monday. Des came in the office earlier than usual. A bunch of mail had just arrived from the mailroom for her boss, Mr Zultan. The intern who delivered it was complaining because it was a thick pile—almost a foot high—and it wasn't easy to carry around even with a cart.

As a manner of routine, Des opened the letters one by one to sort them, giving priority to the important and urgent. Imagining the mails as fan mails, the bubbly Des would open each envelope with excitement and eagerness.

There were letters to the editor from readers expressing their opinion about a news item, a columnist's opinion or an issue, letter complaints from subscribers about their delayed newspaper subscriptions, letter inquiries on career opportunities from job seekers as well as On-the-job-training (OJT) openings from journalism students, letters from the board of directors, congratulatory letters from friends, solicitation letters seeking sponsorships, and more.

Then she noticed an odd-looking letter with Mr Zultan's name written in blood-red ink. What could it be?

Des opened the envelope and was taken aback by the cryptic message inscribed:

STOP THE STORY OR GET A HOLE IN YOUR CHEST.

Sensing a hard item was enclosed, she shook the envelope and out fell a bullet, which made her almost slip from her chair with a yelp. Luckily she was able to keep her balance and composure.

With quivering fingers, she turned the letter inside out for further clues and found a post-script written on the back:

ON SECOND THOUGHT, THE BULLET ALREADY FOUND ITS MARK ON YOUR COAT. YOU MIGHT NOT BE AS LUCKY NEXT TIME.

There were punched-out pieces of fabric glued to the letter. The message was unsigned.

The red-inked letter sent a shiver down Des's spine. Her mind was racing, trying to think straight. She looked at the clock. It was only half past seven in the morning. Mr Zultan wasn't due to arrive in the office until ten.

'Good,' she told herself. She needed more time to comprehend what was going on and think of how she would respond to this predicament. Her boss wasn't an easy man to approach, so she needed to plan out how to say and when to say her spiel. Timing was just as essential as the message.

Aside from being a difficult man, Zultan also hated bad news. And a death threat may be the most difficult news to deliver.

Because of this, numerous questions began to form in her head:

How will I inform him that he has received a death threat?

Should I say it when he comes in?

Or should I say it after he takes his morning coffee?

Should I say it plainly out loud?

Or should I whisper it to downplay its effect?

Then, a morbid thought crossed her mind.

What if the killers were already watching us from outside?

What if a sniper shoots a bullet through the window?

What if the killers intercept him on his way to the office?

With this thought, Des decided that it was best to call Mr Zultan ASAP to warn him. She had set his number on speed dial.

'Hello? Who's this?' barked a grumpy voice on the other line.

'Good morning Sir, it's Des. Sorry to wake you,' she said apologetically.

'You know I get up late because I work long hours at night. This better be urgent or I'll … '

Des was panicking and cut her boss mid-sentence unintentionally. She blurted out without thinking. 'Sir, I just received a death threat in the mail today.'

'What?' Zultan exclaimed. He couldn't believe what he was hearing.

Des was fumbling to find the right words. 'No, Sir. What I mean is that I did not receive a death threat. You received a death threat. I just happened to be here to receive it for you.'

'Will you please slow down a bit and put your act together?' Zultan ordered, trying to calm Des into speaking more coherently.

Des began to fan herself, took several deep breaths to calm herself down and then continued. 'Sir, a letter for you arrived in the mail today. It contained a bullet and a piece of fabric as a warning. The letter says, "Stop the story or get a hole in your chest." There is also a post-script about the bullet already finding its mark on your coat. It was unsigned. I'm sorry, but I don't have any clues as to what story they were referring to.'

Zultan was shocked beyond words. There was a momentary lull in the conversation before he was able to react.

'Did you say there was a bullet and a piece of fabric enclosed in the letter?' he asked, to check if he had heard it right.

'Yes, Sir,' said Des.

There was a long silence as he let the reality of the threat sink in.

'Sir, are you still there? Are you okay, Sir?' Des asked. She was worried that her boss might be in shock or having a heart attack.

'Yes, I'm here. Things are just getting too complicated. Just give me a few seconds. I'm thinking how to proceed,' replied Mr Zultan. Verbalizing what he intended to do and doing it afterwards had proved to be effective in helping him rationalize any situation.

A few seconds more and Zultan was able to compose himself.

'Des, I'll come down immediately to the office. Please call the head of security and Mr Dipasupil to meet me in my office in thirty minutes. Thanks for your help, Des.'

Various scenarios were playing inside Des's mind. She wanted to cover all grounds.

'Sir, will you be driving by yourself? I can request for an escort,' she suggested.

'No need, Des. I'll be okay.'

'How about a bulletproof vest, Sir? You should wear one, just to be safe.'

Zultan was smiling on the other line. 'I appreciate your concern, Des. Don't worry about me. And don't panic. It's part of our job to get threats like this.'

As Zultan put down the phone after the call ended, he couldn't help but feel heavy inside. As a journalist and editor, he prided himself for always upholding the truth no matter what. Because of this, he always asked his reporters not to be biased in reporting but to go out and seek the truth, to present not just one side but other sides of the story too, so that the reader had the benefit of the whole picture.

While he had received death threats in the past, he felt that this was different. The incidents that unfolded every day since the story came out on the front page were getting messier and messier. It had been giving him headaches during the day in the office and depriving him of sleep at night. Even weekends failed to offer him the much-needed rest. He was starting to feel the heat.

Zultan got up from the bed and looked out his bedroom window. He saw his wife in the garden, pruning the plants. She was an early riser unlike him.

He walked to the coat hanger standing in the room. Two of his coats were hanging there. He examined the coats for any holes. As he feared, there were indeed holes in them.

The letter in the mail was a valid threat and sent by someone who was sure to carry out the task.

As with the threats that he had received in the past, he always asked for the assistance of the police. Now, with the police on the other side of the fence, he resolved to discuss the matter with Mr Dipasupil and the building's head of security.

Seeing his wife outside the house, tending the plants, totally unaware of the danger, he sighed. His daughters and grandchildren were coming to visit tomorrow afternoon for a family barbecue. It was meant to be a joyous celebration of their thirty-eighth anniversary.

Is the dead boy really worth all the trouble?

Chapter Nineteen

Strange Thing Called Power

Imagine when you have power and influence and you have the world at your bidding, what would you do?

—PO1 Gilbert Ryan Guillermo

PO1 Gilbert Ryan Guillermo was new in the service. Mild-mannered and polite, he was put in charge of the station's police blotter—the daily register of all crime incident reports, complaints, official summary of arrests made, and other activities of worth in the police station. He was also tasked to handle all inquiries received at the front desk, through the telephone and by email.

Young and idealistic, he wanted to be a role model to his fellowmen and women in uniform by upholding the agency's motto: 'To serve and protect' while adding, 'especially the young, the voiceless, and the powerless', to give it a deeper meaning and draw it closer to his heart that was yearning to make a difference.

He wanted to preserve the image of the police as persons of authority, skill and integrity whom people could run to for help and protection.

Growing up, he was no stranger to various forms of oppression, physical or otherwise. As an orphan, he was taken in by a distant relative, a cousin of his mother who took pity on him. He was given work as a farm hand on their mango plantation in exchange for his education. He attended his classes in the morning and worked on the farm in the afternoon.

He suffered prejudiced treatment from his aunt's husband and his two sons, who made him work longer hours to earn his keep. He would carry baskets of mangoes into the storage houses, then load them into trucks.

His body would cry from extreme exhaustion, but his aunt couldn't do anything but plead for understanding because there was so much work to do on the farm, especially during the harvest season. And she dared not go against her husband, whose family owned the vast farmlands for many generations.

During the times he found it difficult to sleep, he couldn't help but ruminate about how unfortunate his life was. He wondered why he was born poor, why he was orphaned at a young age, why he was powerless and at the mercy of people who didn't care for him.

But before he would completely lose himself in self-loathing, he would pick himself up and ask himself a set of questions: *When will I be able to save enough money? When will I be able to leave this place? When will I be able to chart my own path and live the life I want?*

And the answer that he told himself became his credo and eventually, his source of hope: it's only a matter of time.

As he geared up to finish his secondary education while working on the farm, he witnessed how money dictated power and its manifestation in the relationship between his aunt and her husband. He saw how she had remained dutiful and subservient, content with the small amount she received from her husband for her weekly subsistence. This made him conclude that whoever controlled the purse strings wielded power. But upon reflecting further, he wondered whether he should spend the rest of his days working for money or if he would be better off in pursuit of power.

After finishing high school, he set himself to sail on a day's journey to Manila. He bid his aunt goodbye and applied for a scholarship at the police academy. He was among the lucky ones to be accepted. The long work hours at the farm made him fit and strong. He was able to ace the physical fitness and endurance test without any difficulty. It was as if fate had prepared him for it.

Looking back at the long hours he had spent at the farm, hauling fruit-laden baskets under the scorching sun, enduring cruel treatment, he couldn't help but feel grateful that he hadn't given up. The events in his life, no matter how bitter, added up and moulded him into the person he had become. It reinforced his belief in the higher powers that ruled the universe, that everything happens for a reason.

On his first week at the police station, he received several complaints—against abusive employers who withheld their workers' pay and benefits, pickpockets who were caught red-handed; scammers who hacked into people's social media accounts asking for money or mobile load; thieves who posed as new house maids and were caught (with CCTV footage as evidence); and those who physically and verbally abused women and children. The latter he referred to the Women and Children Protection desk.

There were reports filed on missing persons and missing pets.

There were also disputes among neighbours on issues such as parking space, distressing loud noises, encroaching tree branches and inoperable vehicles blocking the road.

With his good analytical and interpersonal skills, gentle but authoritative voice, and genuine desire to help, he was able to settle these disputes and find a solution that everyone found agreeable.

After six months, he wanted to try fieldwork, since he felt he could do more than just paperwork. So he talked to his supervising officer and asked if there were any available vacancies in other police units.

With the ongoing Oplan Tokhang programme of the government, PO1 Guillermo was transferred to a police unit under the Philippine Drug Enforcement Agency (PDEA), where he was tasked to join a team of anti-illegal drug operatives.

After undergoing several orientation and role-playing sessions, PO1 Guillermo felt he was ready to conduct house visits of those on the drug watch list. He was assigned to team up with a senior officer, SPO2 Santos, a big bearded man with a paunch, who was eight years his senior. Both of them were to report to Police Inspector Dela Cruz, a decorated officer behind the arrest of several notorious gangs.

PO1 Guillermo was excited about his new assignment. Finally, he would see some real action and play an important role. His young heart skipped with innocent delight.

After receiving the revised narcotics list, which according to the PDEA had been verified and signed off, the raiding team arrived in the area. They were looking for the apartment of Eliseo Reyes.

Since the time they had left the station, PO1 Guillermo was pissed off at his co-officer SPO2 Santos, who reeked of alcohol. But what bothered him more was that their commanding officer, Inspector Dela Cruz seemed not to take notice.

There were bystanders near the gate of the compound so PO1 Guillermo took the initiative to ask around for information.

'Good morning! May I know if a certain Eliseo Reyes lives around here?'

One of the men directed him to enquire inside the compound.

Upon entering the gate, they saw a woman washing clothes near a deep well. When they mentioned the name again, she asked them, 'Are you looking for Mang Jun or his son Jun-Jun?'

'How many people with that name live here anyway? If we want to see them all, it's really none of your business,' SPO2 Santos retorted.

The woman frowned at the seemingly rude reply. Nonetheless, she held up her hand filled with soap suds and motioned towards the far end of the row of apartments. 'Their family occupies the largest apartment unit,' she said.

SPO2 Santos immediately walked towards the direction that the woman had pointed out. PO1 Guillermo politely thanked the woman for her help and rushed to keep up with his co-officer. Trailing behind them was Inspector Dela Cruz, who threw his half-consumed cigarette to the ground. 'The party is just getting started,' he whispered.

It was SPO2 Santos who started knocking on the door of the Reyes family's apartment.

'Open the door! This is the police!'

Jun-Jun and his siblings, Princess and Angelo, were surprised to hear the banging. The man's voice sounded harsh and alarming, which scared them so much so that no one wanted to open the door. This angered the officer even more and made him bang louder.

'Open the door or I'll tear this down!'

The children's uncle, Mang Edgar who lived in the next-door apartment, heard the noise. He went out and talked to the police. After being informed that they were looking for Eliseo Reyes whose name was on the drug watch list, Mang Edgar's immediate reaction was to defend his brother.

'Sirs, you must be mistaken because my brother was a good man.'

Tipsy and irritable, SPO2 Santos felt insulted on hearing those words. 'Are you saying we made a mistake? This list was put together by our Intelligence unit and signed-off as accurate by no less than the directors and high-ranking officers of PDEA. This list could make or break a man's life and reputation, do you understand? So we cannot afford to make a mistake with this list,' SPO2 Santos said with a growl.

Mang Edgar turned silent, since he was unable to argue with what the policeman had said.

To ease the growing tension, PO1 Guillermo politely showed Mang Edgar the list of names with signatures of high-ranking police officers as proof.

Seeing his late brother's name on the narco list made Mang Edgar emotional. He was hurt, and he felt insulted. It just wasn't right for the police, or anyone for that matter, to tarnish the good name of his brother. And what hurt him the most was that his brother was long gone and could no longer defend himself against this accusation.

'Are you crying, Sir?' asked PO1 Guillermo when he noticed Mang Edgar's misty eyes.

'Because this list is an injustice. You are accusing my brother of something he did not do. He died a few months ago. And this is an insult to the memory he left behind.'

This irked Police Inspector Dela Cruz. 'Sir, first you accuse us of being mistaken, then you tell us this person is dead! You should have told us that he was dead the moment we asked about him. Who are you fooling?'

Inspector Dela Cruz felt that the family might be trying to hide the suspect. So, he ordered everyone in the compound to line up outside their apartments and say their names aloud.

PO1 Guillermo was starting to feel alarmed because the situation was turning from bad to worse, and it was nothing like what they had practised during their training sessions.

'My name is Eliseo Reyes ...' The moment the tall and lanky boy said his name, SPO2 Santos immediately wrapped his pudgy fingers on the boy's bony wrists without letting him finish his sentence.

PO1 Guillermo knew something was amiss. His co-officers weren't following prescribed procedure in making an arrest.

He grabbed his service pistol and looked at SPO2 Santos with eyes probing for an explanation.

He turned to his commanding officer Inspector Dela Cruz for an answer. But the look he got was all the more disheartening. The sharp look in his eyes was ordering him to stand down.

'We shall escort the young man for questioning about his alleged involvement in the illegal drug trade.'

PO1 Guillermo loosened his grip on his firearm and lowered his hand. He gritted his teeth as he followed his co-officer escort the young man down the road to a lonely spot overshadowed by trees.

He watched as his co-officers began interrogating the boy.

At first SPO2 Santos was calm asking questions but he slowly became irritable. He told the boy that if he confessed, they would help him avail of the drug rehabilitation programme or livelihood programme of the government. But the boy was firm, making SPO2 Santos lose his patience.

'*Hindi ka ba talaga aamin?* (Will you confess or not?)'

'*Maniwala po kayo. Wala po akong alam sa sinasabi ninyo.* (Please believe me. I know nothing of the things that you are accusing me of.)' The boy looked scared. He couldn't give a straight answer to any of the questions. The sight of the gun in the police officer's hands made him jumpy. '*Maawa po kayo. Pauwiin nyo na po ako. May test pa po ako bukas.* (I beg you, please let me go. I have a test tomorrow.)' The boy begged as he began to cry.

After another round of questions, Inspector Dela Cruz finally told SPO2 Santos to stop the interrogation.

'*Mukhang hindi natin mapaaamin itong bata.* (I don't think we can make this boy confess.)'

SPO2 Santos blurted out. '*Pero Sir, paano yung "no zero day" na insentib?* (But Sir, what about the "no zero day" incentive?)'

'*Itikom mo yang bunganga mo!* (You keep your mouth shut!)' retorted Inspector Dela Cruz before turning to the boy who was crying. '*Takbo na at huwag kang lilingon.* (Run and don't look back.)'

As Jun-Jun ran in the direction of his house. SPO2 Santos who was still half-drunk, took out his gun.

'Run, boy, run!' SPO2 Santos hollered like a maniac and began to playfully shoot at the boy, who tried to run faster.

PO1 Guillermo was aghast. He held his gun and pointed it at SPO2 Santos in an attempt to make him stop shooting.

But it was too late. A bullet had hit the boy in the leg.

PO1 Guillermo ran to where the boy had fallen and saw blood oozing out from the boy's leg. The boy was hysterical and crying loudly because of the pain. PO1 Guillermo tried to calm the boy and put him in a comfortable position. Then he got a clean handkerchief and applied pressure on the wound to help stop the bleeding.

When he turned around, he saw Inspector Dela Cruz talking down on SPO2 Santos. There was an exasperated look on his face, mixed with a look of disappointment.

'You never really learn, do you?' he said, trying to control his anger and keep his voice low. 'I told you not to drink before a raid. It makes you trigger-happy.'

'I'm sorry Uncle. I couldn't control my fingers when I got excited.'

Turning to PO1 Guillermo, Inspector Dela Cruz called out, 'Santos did not mean to hurt the boy. The shooting was an accident.'

The boy's relatives and neighbours arrived at the scene.

When the ambulance arrived, the medical team lauded PO1 Guillermo for administering first aid on the boy. But when they carried the boy to the ambulance, they discovered that he had also been hit in the groin. The boy was weak and had already lost a lot of blood.

Inspector Dela Cruz was shaking his head in disbelief. A simple interrogation had turned into a shooting frenzy and now innocent blood could ruin his track record that took him many years to build. He was only two years short of retirement. He couldn't allow something like this to tarnish his good name.

He planned to call the general and explain the whole incident in detail. If worse came to worst, he would invoke the President's own words: 'As long as a police officer is fulfilling his duty under the "Oplan Tokhang" anti-drug campaign, he shall be absolved and protected by the law.'

But Inspector Dela Cruz had another problem. The rookie officer Guillermo saw the whole incident. If someone tried to find out the truth, it could be Guillermo's words against his. He sighed in frustration. The young officer looked smart and promising, unlike his nephew SPO2 Santos who seemed to have lost his wits to alcohol. He wondered for how long he could cover up his nephew's dirty tracks.

He also felt sorry to let the young officer go. He would have to find an excuse to transfer him to another unit. It would be safer that way.

'Guillermo, you can escort the boy to the hospital. Santos and I will take care of this mess and inform the general about this accidental shooting.'

PO1 Guillermo was dismayed that his commanding officer kept referring to the whole incident as a shooting accident and appeared to be more concerned about clearing his name than telling the truth.

He thought about the power play that he had witnessed at the farm of his aunt, and realized how power could blind people, making them see only themselves and regard those around them as a notch less important or even insignificant.

Seeing how his commanding officer twisted the truth to clear his name of the blame, he attributed it again to the corrupting nature of power and how it could make people pass a lie as truth to save themselves and let others take the blame.

PO1 Guillermo had understood that like money, power too is a strange thing. It blinds the eye, corrupts the heart, and numbs the senses.

Chapter Twenty

The Coat Mystery

People frown at those who are too interested in others. They label them as observant, curious, prying and nosy. But sometimes, being observant, curious, prying and nosy can also mean someone cares enough to look. Sometimes it can also save the day.

—Des

That Monday was perhaps the longest day that Zeke had ever spent at the office. His meeting with Mr Zultan and the building's chief security officer lasted for over four hours.

Zultan brought out his coats—one was dark grey and the other was brown—and showed them the holes that were punched at the hemlines. They were almost unnoticeable if one wasn't really looking hard enough.

'It appears that the one responsible for ripping holes in your coats was able to stand close enough to you to do this,' the chief security officer surmised while nibbling on a toothpick. 'The person could be standing in line behind you, maybe at a vending machine, a coffee shop, in a train or at a lotto outlet.'

'No,' Zultan curtly disagreed. 'I don't usually go out of my office for coffee because we have our own expresso machine. I don't buy from a vending machine, I don't ride trains, and I have long quit trying my luck at lotto.'

The chief security officer gave out a sigh, with a look that said—*this is harder than we think.*

His secretary Des quickly stepped in and lay a tray of brewed coffee and some pastries for the three gentlemen.

'Or maybe the person could be standing next to you inside the lift,' Zeke suggested.

'Still no,' said Zultan. He frowned at the suggestion since he seldom rode a lift with other people.

But Zeke's suggestion did not sit well with the chief security officer who was slightly offended.

The man raised his brow behind his large spectacles. 'Are you insinuating that the suspect was able to breach our security and get inside the building premises? You're making us look like we're not doing what we are supposed to do.'

Zeke raised his hands in surrender. 'I'm not accusing anyone. I'm just letting my thoughts run freely. I mean, we have to identify that one instance when the suspect was able to come near Zultan, close enough to punch a hole in his coat without him knowing it.'

Des was on her way out with the empty tray when she caught on to some bits of the conversation. It set her inquisitive mind to work immediately.

There hadn't been many visitors to Zultan's office in the past few days. Also, he seldom left his office to go out, say, to a deli, for snacks. So who could have darted close enough to get a sample fabric off her boss's coat?

Every night before retiring to bed, Des used to write a short paragraph in her journal about something that transpired during the day. It could be something new or strange, especially something that was out of the normal order of things.

She checked her journal entries for the past week.

Two odd incidents had taken place. One was an encounter with a window cleaner, who knocked on Zultan's office window as he hung in a harness from outside. Since the windows were sealed, his voice was a bit muted, and he had to motion to her to tell her that he had found a hole under the window and asked her to call the housekeeping department and send someone to fix it.

What surprised her was that as soon as she put down the phone after calling housekeeping, a loud knock was heard at the door. She found it odd because it was too fast to be true, like the man was just outside her door the whole time, waiting for her to get off the phone.

The repair man looked nothing out of the ordinary. He was dressed in a coverall suit and carried a toolbox.

She then escorted the man inside Zultan's office and watched him mix a small packet of what looked like white cement and patched the hole in the wall with it.

Then the phone on her desk rang so she went out of Zultan's room momentarily to answer it. It was a wrong number.

When she stepped inside the room again, she caught the repair man holding Zultan's coat. He was in the act of returning the coat to the coat hanger.

'The coat accidentally dropped. I was just putting it back,' the man said.

Des specifically remembered fussing over the incident, saying she wouldn't want to get Zultan's coats soiled since the man was handling cement.

She got the coats from the man and hung them on the hanger herself.

Then the man painted the patch on the wall with the same colour of paint as the rest of Zultan's office, making it hardly noticeable.

She vividly remembered her own remark: 'That's the quickest fix-it job I have ever seen!'

And then the man's demeanour changed. Guilt was written all over his face like he was caught red-handed. After a few seconds, he was able to come to his senses.

'The hole is fixed, Ma'am. If there is anything else you need, just dial housekeeping.'

Then, quick as a snap, the man stepped out the door and was gone.

Thinking back, Des assumed that Mr Fix-it could have punched holes in the coats when she went out of the room to answer the phone call. She had even caught him red-handed holding the coat as he was putting it back on the coat hanger.

It was just an assumption, but it had a strong probability of being true, since the two elements of the mystery were present at the scene: strangers and Mr Zultan's coats.

She wanted so much to help solve the mystery of how the coats had holes in them. Mr Fix-it was just a theory but she couldn't sit still at her desk. She had a hard time concentrating on her work. She knew that she couldn't possibly last the entire day with her mouth shut trying to hold it in. It felt like an important piece of information that she must disclose.

So, Des summoned up all her courage and knocked on Zultan's door.

'It's open,' Zultan roared as usual.

'Sirs,' Des addressed the three men, her heart thumping inside her chest, 'I have some important information that I think you should know.'

'Yes, go on,' said Zultan leaning forward on his desk.

Zeke and the chief security officer put down their coffee cups to give their full attention to Des.

'Sirs, I overheard you wondering about the holes in Mr Zultan's coats and how someone could have possibly stood so close to him to be able to punch holes in them without him noticing it ... '

The three men sat still in their seats, listening intently with bated breaths, waiting for her to finish.

'I have strong reason to believe that the culprits posed as a window cleaner and a Mr Fix-it from housekeeping. Last week, a window cleaner knocked from outside the window and told me to call housekeeping to fix a hole that he had found under Mr Zultan's window. The weird thing is, the repair man was instantly at my door right after I called housekeeping to do the repair.

'Then, when I stepped out to answer a phone call on my desk, I got back just in time to catch the repair man holding one of the coats. He said that the coats had accidentally dropped to the floor, and he was just returning them. But my intuition says he's lying. And my intuition is seldom wrong.

'So you see, the culprits could have punched the holes while the coats were hanging inside his office, and not while he was wearing them, as you previously thought,' Des concluded.

There was silence for a few moments before Zeke spoke up. 'Thanks for that information, Des. I think those people were just trying to intimidate us and the most they could do was break into the office and stab at coats on a hanger.'

Zultan praised his secretary for speaking up. 'I think that was very brave and conscientious of you, Des. I truly appreciate you telling us about this incident.'

'Anything to help, Sir,' said Des.

'You might want to consider a career in the future as an investigator,' added the chief of security.

Des blushed, feeling light and rosy inside as she went out the door.

Chapter Twenty-one

Revelation and Help

Asking for help is not a sign of weakness. It's a humble recognition that we need one another.

—Kit Dimalanta

Friday nights at Conchita's had always been a welcome respite for Zeke, but for Kit it was more than that. It was a once-a-week private affair, a midnight appointment of sorts, a time to beat one's drum and rave about 'successes' or the good things that transpired at work, a chance to blow off steam and rant about 'failures' or the things that didn't turn out well as planned, and most of all, it was a moment to be with the person who magnified every success making it worth celebrating and downplayed every failure making it less painful and frustrating.

Kit came early as always. She would spend some quiet time to be by herself, just sitting near the pond in the al fresco dining area, to compose her thoughts and think about the things she would tell Zeke.

A lot of things had transpired that week. Then there was the strange envelope that someone had dropped at her office at the fire station. She found it strange that nobody at the station saw the person who delivered it. It was addressed to Zeke. She would hand it over to Zeke when he came.

Zeke arrived at the restaurant shortly after midnight. He looked tired like he hadn't had any sleep.

'Sorry to be late ... as always.'

'Hi! What happened to you? Have you tried looking at your face in the mirror? You look horrible.'

Zeke just smiled and said, 'You know how I'm married to my job—can't live with it, can't live without it.'

Kit drew closer to get a whiff. True enough, Zeke reeked of alcohol. His eyes were droopy with sleep.

'Have you been drinking?'

'Took a few swigs with Mr Z in his office. He's feeling a bit low so I kept him company for a while ... By the way, how was your date with Mr God of Thunder?'

Kit felt her emotions shift. She was amused that Zeke cared to ask.

'It's a no-go. We only went out twice then he wanted me to go back to the US with him. It's too hasty. I had to let it go.'

'I agree that it's too hasty. He should have waited for the third date,' Zeke said with a snigger.

'You're crazier when you're drunk, Zeke.'

Kit found it strange that Zeke would care to drink. Something must really be off.

'You're not a drinker. You only drink ginger ale. What is going on, Zeke?' Kit demanded an explanation.

Zeke just smiled and looked at her, trying to keep his eyes open.

Looking at Zeke, Kit realized that talking to a drunk would be a complete waste of time.

'Never mind. Let's just go home. I'll drive you.'

Zeke shook his head in protest. 'No, not a good idea.'

Then she remembered the strange envelope. She took it out from her bag and handed it to Zeke.

'By the way, someone dropped this at my office. It's for you. Maybe they thought we're related.' Kit scoffed at her own words.

The envelope was an ordinary letter envelope. His name was written on its face in bold red ink.

Zeke was hesitant at first to open it in front of Kit but decided to do it anyway.

'The heck with it,' he said under his breath.

It was a letter with a cryptic message, similar to what Zultan had received. It read:

STOP THE STORY. OR YOUR HEART WILL BURN.

It was unsigned.

Zeke folded the letter and placed it back inside the envelope. He didn't want to look affected in front of Kit.

'Can we get some coffee? I need to clear my head,' he said massaging his neck, trying to act sober.

A waiter was quick to get their order. Kit added some cinnamon rolls to match the coffee.

'Hey, care to share what's in the letter?' Kit asked casually. 'Is it from a secret admirer?'

'It's nothing, just a prank, trying to scare me out of my skin.'

'What does it say?'

'It says, "Stop the story or … "' Zeke suddenly hesitated. A few seconds of silence had already lapsed but his mind was still blank.

'Or what? You can tell me,' Kit quipped.

'It says "Stop the story or you'll get heartburn." Funny, right? Maybe they meant something else, like stop writing too many articles or you'll get acid reflux.'

'Acid reflux?' Kit asked with a confused look.

'Yeah, it's another term for heartburn. It's when acid rises up from your stomach and irritates your oesophagus.'

'I know what acid reflux means! What I mean is, I don't get why someone would write you a letter warning you about getting acid reflux. It has to mean something else.'

Zeke fell silent. He was trying to downplay the letter's message, even adding a playful spin to it. But Kit's insistence was hard to shake off. Given her training at the police academy, she had always been headstrong, wanting to get involved in solving every problem that came her way.

Zeke realized his predicament had just gotten more complicated. How could he keep her out of it? He could seldom fake anything with Kit because she always seemed to see through his cover.

'You know very well how we get these prank letters. Some are funny, some are scary. Some are downright annoying like this one.'

Kit's eyes narrowed, her brows scrunched, not quite convinced.

The waiter arrived just in time to provide the much-needed break. He brought two lattes in dainty white cups and two warm cinnamon rolls on matching white plates. Forks and knives were set alongside.

The tension made Zeke feel hungry all of a sudden. He didn't realize he was *that* hungry until he found himself finishing the cinnamon roll in three big bites. Kit just looked on.

Then he took a big gulp of the steaming brew, too late to realize that it was piping hot. He let out a cry of pain, trying to blow out some air to cool his scalded tongue.

Kit wasn't amused. More so, she could see that Zeke was despairing over something. 'Zeke, I think whoever sent that letter is threatening you. Care to share what's really going on? Perhaps I can help?'

But Zeke was hesitant. Whoever sent the letter was dangerous, serious about their demand. They did a background check on Kit and knew how important she was to him. They got her address and probably knew her schedule too, all her comings and goings.

The controversial article published in *The Manila Daily Star* had shaken up the police hierarchy. Her life could be in danger too. It was a risk he just couldn't take. He felt a knot in his stomach just thinking about the possibility of losing her. He couldn't imagine having to go through the day without her in it. But on the contrary, her training at the police academy might even help them with whatever threats they were facing. Besides, he had kept her in the dark for so long about many things in his life. Maybe this time, for a change, he should let her in.

He felt bad about taking her for granted. He regretted wasting all the years they spent together, yapping senselessly about being content with their present lives. He wondered why they never talked about each other's dreams or what they wanted for the future. How he wished he could find an appropriate occasion to tell her how he felt. Why did it have to be this way? Surely they didn't need a life-threatening crisis like this to jolt them into realizing what they really wanted to do with their lives. Or did they?

Aside from Kit, there was Jun-Jun's family to worry about too. His anonymous eyewitness, Yumi Salvacion, had informed him that some police officers had started visiting Jun-Jun's wake in an attempt to find out who had been releasing information to the media. They were clearly intimidating family members and preventing them from making further statements or interviews.

There was a lot on his plate right now.

Summing up all his courage, Zeke told Kit everything there was to know regarding the issue stirred up by Jun-Jun's article. Despite the death threat he had received, he felt that he should go and finish the follow-up stories, which would be a big exposé. But first, he needed to get past Zultan, who wasn't keen on publishing another story.

'So, what do you think?' he asked Kit.

Kit smiled, her countenance the same. The look of confidence and determination never left her eyes.

'If it's a war they want, we won't take this sitting down. You do what you have to do. I'm getting reinforcements.'

Chapter Twenty-two

The Follow-up Story

Shine like lights to the world as you hold on to the word of truth.
—Zechariah 'Zeke' Dipasupil

The clock read 4:33 p.m. Zeke had just finished writing the article detailing the circumstances surrounding the boy's death at the hands of policemen based on his interviews with Yumi and Mang Edgar. It was written as hard news, told in a straightforward manner bereft of emotion.

As soon as Zeke finished the final sentence, his eyes were misty. He felt resentment for the abuse done to the innocent. He felt regret for the life lost, a long string of 'what-could-have-been's in a boy's life erased just like that.

Zeke was angry at the injustice and the prejudiced treatment that Jun-Jun had received because he was young, weak and helpless.

Then the red-inked letter caught his eye. It was folded on his table. He had forgotten all about it because he was completely preoccupied with writing the article and finishing it before the 5:00 p.m. deadline. He was reminded of the stern warning and its subtle reference to Kit. He grimaced just thinking about how ugly the situation had become.

Who are these people anyway? Haven't they done enough damage already? Why do they want to hurt more people?

'The heck with it,' he muttered to himself. He wouldn't let things get any uglier. He wouldn't allow another wave of injustice to happen. He wouldn't let these perpetrators of evil stop this article from getting printed in the next day's paper.

He thought about the sacrifices he had made to bring the story this far.

Realizing that he was already deep in the game, he thought about writing a second article to present another angle to the issue.

So, he researched and gathered data on the number of drug-related crimes and deaths that were recorded since the President started the Oplan Tokhang programme. He included the demographics of the victims and their communities, the localities in which they lived, and the number of deaths per day, per week, and in four weeks' time. It was a chilling presentation of facts on the ongoing anti-drug war with a surprisingly high death toll.

Zeke knew Zultan was also deeply troubled by the red-inked letter that he had received a few days back. His boss would definitely hesitate to publish his articles. Or worse, he might berate him and tell him that he's out of his mind for even attempting to fan the flames surrounding the controversial issue.

But there might be a saving grace: an exclusive interview with an eyewitness was something hard to find. And for a sensible editor, it would be hard to resist publishing it. He would just have to guide Zultan to the light.

So Zeke resolved to see Zultan personally in his office to present the two articles he had written. He hoped and prayed that the new information he was able to collect would merit his boss's approval for publication. And given the growing public interest on the story, as evidenced by the growing number of calls and online inquiries received at the office, he might just request for a larger space on the front page, and in so doing, create a statement for the red-ink letter senders that they weren't afraid to make the truth known. He'd work with the layout artists to create a headline in big, bold letters, just to make sure the story would be hard for anyone to miss.

Upon arriving at Zultan office, he was met by Des, who was warm and amiable as always but was quick to warn him: 'Mr Zultan's not in his best mood today. He's been screaming at almost everybody who goes into his office, including me. I hope what you have right there would be music to his ears.'

'I hope so too,' Zeke replied before closing the door behind him.

As expected, Zultan wasn't smiling after reading the two articles. 'What's all this crap, Mr Dipasupil?'

'It's not crap. It's the truth, Sir,' Zeke replied plainly. He was used to his boss's surly demeanour.

'You want me to publish this, saying this boy died from police brutality? We might as well be shot dead in our beds and our company shut down for libel.'

'Sir, I have evidence to prove that this was what actually happened that night. I have a witness—no, make that two witnesses, or maybe more if you let me find them.'

But Zultan wasn't smiling. The furrows in his brows had become more apparent. 'Zeke, you are a brilliant journalist. But the problem with you is, you–don't–listen. We both received death threats! I told you to let this issue rest but you never listened. Instead you come up with not just one but two articles! Are you trying to taunt them? You are brilliant but stubborn and foolish.'

Zeke retorted. 'Sir, I just happened to stumble upon the witnesses, like fate led me to them or them to me. I did not go—'

'Don't give me that shit!' Zultan's booming voice seemed to reverberate through the office walls. 'You shouldn't be in the boy's house attending his wake in the first place. You have no business being there!'

Zeke felt his emotions rising but was able to contain them, letting out a loud sigh. 'All right. All right! But for the record, I did not drive to the area looking for the boy's address. I was there on an errand and just realized it wouldn't hurt to pay my last respects.'

'You know what you're doing? You're rubbing salt into the wound. God knows if tomorrow we might be swimming in our own blood,' Zultan exclaimed with a look of disappointment, regret and fear.

'All right. If you find my expositions too scandalous and upsetting, then at least we should release an update, no matter how short. We owe it to the public. Where is the reporter that you assigned earlier to do the follow-up story?'

At that point, Zultan gave a look of exasperation mixed with surrender. 'The reporter called in to say he couldn't come up with anything new. He said the police that he interviewed didn't provide anything other than what was already reported. The mother of the dead boy was also uncooperative. She was angry at the police and at the media.'

Zeke felt vindicated. 'So does that mean my articles will finally see the light?'

'No! I'm still not publishing that. We have enough troubles of our own. Go home and get some sleep,' Zultan said sternly. 'I think I need some myself.'

But Zeke wasn't about to give up. 'Sir, when we got the truth on our side, there's nothing to be afraid of.'

'That will only happen in a perfect world. In reality, people will tell their version of the truth, the one that works to their advantage. Sometimes something is accepted as true because someone powerful said so. And the weak can do nothing about it.'

'But the world deserves to know the truth.'

Zultan turned silent. He looked at Zeke in a fatherly way, as if begging for a sliver of understanding. 'Zeke, you know me. I've always believed in you and what you stand for. But you are treading on dangerous grounds. Call me a coward, but I'm afraid the articles you wrote might backfire on us. I could feel that the threats are real this time.'

'Sir, you also know me,' replied Zeke. 'I always stand by the truth regardless of the consequences. I knew I was signing for a death sentence when I took this job … If we let fear paralyse us because we are threatened and we fear retaliation, then we ourselves become perpetrators of half-truths and injustice. It is our duty to seek the truth and make it known … and we owe it to those who lost their lives.'

Zultan could no longer argue with Zeke. He let out a long tired sigh. Besides, he couldn't disagree with those parting words said so eloquently.

'To hell with those bastards who killed that boy and others who were innocent! Let's run your stories. Both of them!'

* * *

The next day, the detailed account of Jun-Jun's death at the hands of abusive law enforcers landed on the front page of *The Manila Daily Star*. The banner read: 'Eyewitness account: Boy pleaded for his life but shot dead by drug operatives.' It was the much-awaited follow-up story to the controversial news article previously published about a dead boy tagged as a drug runner.

It was picked up by two morning news programmes on TV and five international news agencies. It was reported on several radio news programmes. It was tweeted and re-tweeted by social media influencers. It was all over the news and social media.

It was the topic of discussion at a popular late-night talk show because of the controversy it courted; a high-ranking police general was put on a hot seat. It was totally unprecedented.

The general was a sport and tried to answer the questions from the host, who tried to be amiable. But the phone-in questions from the viewers weren't as forgiving. The general excused himself during an advertisement break and walked out of the show, leaving the host and the show's writers scrambling for something to patch up the remaining air time.

Despite this untoward incident that nobody saw coming, the talk show's ratings went through the roof, much to the delight of the show's producers.

The detailed story about Jun-Jun's death somewhat confirmed what people had long feared—the anti-drug programme of the government had become a bloodbath, where operatives failed to fulfil the original objective of the programme, which was to talk to and persuade those involved in drugs and help them kick the habit to reform their lives. Instead, the victims were being perceived as plagues of society—hopeless—and better off eradicated.

The anti-drug war had also become a vehicle for policemen to abuse their authority over those who are powerless. The indiscriminate killings were clear violations of the right to life. It was reminiscent of the dark years of Martial Law with police brutality rearing its ugly head again. But with one difference this time—a strong and vital exception—the modern-day media and press were unshackled and had the power to publicize, criticize and expose the truth, even if egoists found it too painful to accept or sceptics found it too hard to believe.

* * *

Aling Benilda had been resting in her room for the past two days. Her blood pressure had shot up to 200/90 ever since several policemen were seen outside the compound gate, trying to ask people if any members of the press or media had been conducting interviews with the family.

She had been trying to remain strong for her two other children, Princess and Angelo. But the presence of the police had been quite distressing.

When her husband, Jun, died a few months ago, she had found a receipt for a three-months' rent to a columbarium vault while rummaging through his things. She wondered if it was a foreboding or if her husband knew of his impending death. But upon checking the vault, she found that it contained her mother's cremated ashes, which led to her discovery of the unexplained cash inside the urn in their house.

Then, her son Jun-Jun was killed. The string of unfortunate events and unexplained discoveries was weighing on her mind. Two deaths in the family within a year's time were too much for an old woman like her to bear. She couldn't help but worry over their future; she couldn't possibly leave her two children and work abroad again.

As in the past, when she found no one to turn to for help, she turned to prayer. And indeed, she found comfort and solace in praying to the Santo Niño in the old stampitas that she kept in her wallet.

She pressed the stampita to her heart, closed her eyes, and prayed to the Santo Niño for strength, protection and a much-needed miracle.

Then, she heard it—a knock on the door. Her daughter, Princess, peeped in, saying there were visitors wanting to see her. The older woman felt an overwhelming feeling of peace wash over her, like her prayer was answered.

When she went out of her room to meet the visitors, she recognized Zeke. He greeted her while handing over a copy of the morning newspaper. She received the paper with trembling hands and couldn't help the tears from falling as she slowly read the banner story: 'Eyewitness account: Boy pleaded for his life but shot dead by drug operatives', which detailed how Jun-Jun was killed as per an anonymous eyewitness.

'How did you—?' Aling Benilda was at a loss for words.

'We're here to tell the world what really happened—no matter the consequences,' said Zeke. 'There are a lot of other victims out there who might also have similar stories but weren't able to tell them.'

Zeke introduced Kit and her firefighter associates from the local fire department. The men were tall and big and burly, but with smiling and friendly faces.

'These are my associates,' said Kit quite proudly. 'They will keep vigil at Jun-Jun's wake to keep the peace and ensure no policemen bothers you.'

'Thank you, thank you …' Aling Benilda said in between sobs. Princess and Angelo were by her side consoling her. They had just witnessed the biggest miracle.

Chapter Twenty-three

Dead Man Talking

As long as you are alive and hopeful, things can change and miracles can happen.

—Senator Lustro

Amid the controversial issues surrounding the government's nationwide anti-drug campaign, the nation was gearing up for the forthcoming national elections.

The campaign period had started. The news coverage on TV and print were heavy on the candidates' campaign trail. The senatorial race had sixty candidates aspiring to fill the twenty-four senatorial positions. The vice-presidential race had eight candidates trying to outdo and outperform one another, while the presidential race had ten, vying for the highest position in the whole archipelago.

With the election campaign going in full swing, various candidates began to organize their political rallies, participate in various debates, and travel to various cities including far-flung areas to reach out to voters across the country.

Depending on their campaign managers, the candidates employed various strategies to win the hearts of voters. In such campaign rallies, candidates would sing and dance to enamour the naïve and gullible citizens. In addition to providing entertainment, the candidates also made use of these face-to-face encounters to roll out platforms and win people's hearts before election day.

Among the vice-presidential candidates, it was Senator Lustro who was leading in the surveys. He had already served two terms as senator. Now, he felt he was ready and ripe to occupy the second-highest position in the land.

Though devious, witty and a sweet talker, Senator Lustro was also a man of letters. But with his hectic schedule and various off-the-record dealings, he had no time to sit down and write. So he opted to hire a ghostwriter to do his speeches and write his weekly newspaper column. And he didn't just hire any writer for the job; he wanted the best and the brightest to put words into his mouth and reflect the inner workings of his mind eloquently on paper.

Zeke had opened a new account and funnelled the money he earned into charitable organizations, particularly those that helped indigent children go to school. These children came from areas with the highest poverty rates in the country, such as Sulu, Basilan, Agusan del Sur, Cotabato City, Sarangani, Tawi-tawi and Zamboanga del Norte. Zeke had signed up as an anonymous donor, following the moral code not to blow a trumpet to announce his good deeds.

The senator's money also funded his quirky smoking habit, which helped him think things out. His mother had chastised him against smoking early on when she caught him trying to smoke at the back of their house. She would say that though smoking often started out as mere curiosity, it could become an addiction. It would only 'burn' his money and leave him bankrupt. Thus, getting a benefactor somewhat helped him get rid of the guilty feeling.

With the controversial issue of the dead boy weighing down on his shoulders, Zeke found it extremely difficult to continue his ghostwriting escapade. He wanted out.

But he knew the senator wouldn't be pleased with his decision. But what could he do? He barely had any sleep in the past several days. He couldn't concentrate. He couldn't think things through even after smoking his 'thinking stick' at his favourite thinking spot.

He looked horrible on the outside but inside he felt worse.

Then, he thought of the children. Who would support their education if the funds stopped? There would be other donors, of course. Maybe he could downsize a bit and continue supporting a few scholars with his own money? A few thousand pesos a month could at least provide meals, books and allowance. Maybe he could also help support them as a volunteer? Since he mostly worked in the afternoon until midnight, his mornings were almost always free. He would just have to give up a few hours of sleep. What's a little sacrifice on his part for the sake of the children? Surely he could do that.

With his decision to quit, Zeke felt a peaceful feeling wash over him. It was a feeling he had not felt in a long while. It was a feeling akin to his cloistered life inside the seminary, where no noise could penetrate its walls. It was the same feeling that he felt as a boy walking near the sea with his mother. It also brought back memories of his time sitting in Chapel Hill, waiting silently for God's voice.

With that, he felt his spirit rejuvenated. He resolved to complete all the campaign materials that the senator needed for his election campaign sorties and provincial roadshows: slogans and speeches; statistical data on economic and political landscapes; sample Q&As for interviews and debates; witty copies for billboard signages, newspaper ads and merchandising; and flyers and comic books. He was thankful that the songs and promotional jingles weren't included in his tasks!

One afternoon, just before going to the office, he decided to drop by Senator Lustro's office, unannounced.

The senator welcomed him warmly into his office, smiling the whole time, making his craggy face appear less repulsive.

'What a pleasant surprise,' said the senator. 'Please take a seat. Allow me to offer you something to drink.'

Immediately, his secretary appeared with a variety of canned drinks—fruit juice, coffee expresso, blended iced teas, beer, cocktail drinks, and ginger ale.

Zeke picked a can of ginger ale and popped its contents into a crystal tumbler. The cold and sweet liquid refreshed him, easing out some of the tension in his chest.

'I got those Baccarat tumblers when I went abroad. My wife was very happy about it. People who weren't really listening thought I was talking about a card game when, in fact, I was talking about a luxury glassware brand.'

Zeke took a closer look at the drinking glasses that the senator was referring to. The designs etched on the crystal were handcrafted, reflecting the skill of a master craftsman.

The senator settled in his chair, which was a Canadian-made dark-brown leather Concorde presidential chair, similar to what US presidents use in the White House.

'So, what can I help you with?'

'Sir,' Zeke began, 'I was … '

Suddenly, the senator cut him off—

'By the way, I've been reading the campaign materials you've sent in a zip file. I've read every single one. And guess what? I couldn't find any errors, not even a typo,' chuckled the Senator. 'Your writing, your research, your punchlines, your slogans— everything is impeccable! I'm very impressed!'

'Thank you, Sir,' Zeke said before turning silent again as he tried to find the right words to open up the topic.

Apparently, the senator wasn't a good listener either. Moreover, he hated pauses, lulls—the silent intervals in a conversation. For him, it dulled the moment, cut the action and broke the momentum.

'So, are you here to ask for a raise? I can give you a raise. That's not a problem. How does an additional PHP300,000 sound to you, on top of your monthly retainer?'

'No, Sir,' Zeke replied meekly. 'I'm not here to ask for a raise. In fact, I am thankful and truly grateful for this opportunity … '

Listening to Zeke, the smile and candour of the senator began to fade as he finally sensed where the conversation was going.

'I'm tendering my resignation, Sir,' Zeke finally said. 'I've completed all my writing assignments and other tasks. But I can't commit any more after the elections. You know how I'm married to my job at the newsroom.'

'So, who's paying you more?' the senator bluntly asked.

'No one. There's just a lot of pressure these days. I can't concentrate on two things … you know how the Bible says that we can't serve two masters … But I'm truly grateful, Sir,' Zeke said.

The senator gave out a laugh. 'Ah yes, you're the author of the biggest anti-drug police scandal. I heard they want to punish you for exposing them. So, I'm like, talking to a dead man right now!'

It wasn't the nicest thing to hear, more so coming from a senator who was running for vice-presidential. But Zeke wasn't surprised at all. He was used to the senator's unethical jokes and harsh comments.

Zeke bid the senator goodbye. As he turned to leave, the senator gave him a piece of advice, which was both unsolicited and surprising.

'If I were you, I would make myself invisible in a crowd. Or, get an escort with a gun when going out. Or, better yet, don't go out at all. And please, hide your lady friend for a while until the storm blows over.'

Chapter Twenty-four

A Second Chance

Not everyone gets a second chance to live. Make sure you cherish every sunrise like it would be your last.

—Zechariah 'Zeke' Dipasupil

It was 5:00 p.m. A small crowd had gathered at the Quirino Grandstand trying to get the best seats with a good view of the stage. It was still early since the campaign rally wasn't due to start until two hours later.

Historically, the Quirino Grandstand had been the traditional venue for many national events held in the capital city of Manila, such as Independence Day celebrations and presidential inaugurations. With a seating capacity of ten thousand, the grandstand was also a site for events such as SEA games' opening ceremonies, papal visits, and other large crowd gatherings.

The campaign rally was organized by the People Power Revolution Party (PPRP), which was Senator Lustro's political party and where he served as its standard bearer.

Zeke mingled with the crowd at the campaign rally, trying to look inconspicuous. He wanted to see how Senator Lustro would deliver the speech he had written. If there was one thing he admired about the senator, it was his ability to memorize his speeches word for word and deliver them flawlessly, with cuts and pauses in the right places, like he was speaking from the heart.

While waiting for the rally to start, Zeke watched as people began arriving by the busloads. Some rode in jeepneys while others were shuttled in overloaded trucks. Their faces were expressionless, and they did not seem to mind standing up during the entire duration of the trip without any personal space like sardines in a can.

As the crowd entered the grandstand, they received flyers, banners, car stickers and posters. They were also given free items for use like folding fans, pens and sun visors.

Many of those who arrived in trucks were shabbily dressed, wearing rubber slippers as if they were taken straight right from their houses without a chance to get properly dressed. They sat on the bleachers fanning themselves, waiting not so much for the programme to start as for the free meals and money promised by the campaign organizers.

Taking all the necessary precaution as advised by Senator Lustro, Zeke wore a ball cap and dark glasses. He also wore a jacket and a scarf around his neck despite the sweltering heat. He wanted to blend in with the crowd. He was sweating under his shirt, made worse by the rising tension that he was feeling.

Zeke never liked crowds. In fact, he would avoid them as much as possible. But today, the crowd was his friend.

Suddenly, Zeke felt his phone vibrating in his pocket. It was Kit.

'Hey, where you at?' she asked, her tone high like a squeak.

Zeke wasn't used to disclosing his location because he liked to keep his whereabouts private. But he remembered the thought he had had last time when he received the death threat letter through Kit. He would try to let Kit into his life, little by little.

'Hi! I'm at the grandstand. I'd like to see how the senator delivers his speech. Then I'm out of here.'

'*Your* speech, you mean?' Kit retorted in a jest.

Zeke had already disclosed his ghostwriting escapade to Kit. At first, she was bug-eyed with surprise since she couldn't imagine Zeke getting involved in a political campaign, much less one for the senator. But her heart melted when Zeke told her about his anonymous donation to help children in Mindanao. He told her it was meant to be anonymous and undisclosed so he could collect his reward in heaven. But not any more.

Then, something came up and Kit had to cut the call short. 'You watch your back and take care. I'll see you Friday. Bye!'

Surveying the crowd, Zeke saw a man walking towards the stage with a small entourage behind him. It was Senator Lustro whose arrival had sent the organizers scrambling in order to start the programme immediately. They were well aware of the senator's busy schedule and his disdain for waiting and inactivity.

Just then, Zeke noticed two suspicious-looking men. One was tall and dark with a stubble. He was standing behind a large speaker. The other was bulkier, wearing a jacket and casually sipping a soda. Both seemed to be discreetly throwing glances in his direction. Instinctively, he felt the need to leave immediately. He weaved his way through the crowd, trying to reach the nearest exit.

Suddenly, a woman ran up to him. She was smiling, dressed as an usher.

'Please go this way, Sir. We are diverting everyone to a new exit.'

In his hurry to get out of the place, Zeke followed in the woman's direction without hesitation. Along the way, another usher met him and directed him again towards another path.

Then, to his surprise, the two men he had seen earlier appeared from behind the crowd of people milling outside the grandstand, flanked him on either side and escorted him into a waiting vehicle. Everything happened so fast he didn't get the chance to say a word—not even a squeak of protest.

* * *

When Zeke came to his senses, he was under some kind of hood. He was bound to a chair. He psyched himself on the horrors that might befall him—truth serum, beatings, water treatment, electrocution, suffocation, strangulation, sexual assault, psychological torture. Nothing could shock him now.

When the hood was removed from his head, what he saw was something he was totally unprepared for—there was a woman gagged and tied to a chair with a sack over her head. Her cries of protests were muffled.

Then, one of the men started to talk. 'Do you like irony? I like ironies. Have you heard of the news today?'

'What news?' asked another.

'The city's fire chief died inside a burning warehouse. It's sad she didn't make it out alive.'

One of the men began to put bundle upon bundle of firewood and other combustible materials around the woman. Then, he poured gasoline over the wood. Then, as a final touch, he poured gasoline over the woman's head still covered with a sack. Then he held up a lighter.

Zeke couldn't stay silent any more. 'What do you want? You already got me. Keep her out of this.'

'Do you know how much damage you've caused? Making us look like we're the bad guys. Can't you see we're trying to get rid of those good-for-nothing people?' the man said with a serious look in his eyes.

'Who are you to judge that they are hopeless and good for nothing? Put them in rehab or jail them. But no one has the right to kill them,' Zeke protested.

The man scoffed at Zeke's words. 'We don't need a complicated process because the President's mandate is very clear. Kill those bastards and make the world safer for our children.'

'What you are doing is against the law, a violation of human rights. Do you know how many people are killed every day in this drug war? Not to mention those that don't make it to the news.'

The man was unfazed. 'I don't blame you. Not everyone will agree with the government's unconventional ways of cleaning up this country of its drug mess.'

Then, the man drew his face closer to Zeke's. It wasn't a special kind of face to behold, but it would remain etched in Zeke's mind for a long time to come.

'Now, are you ready to answer my question so you can save your lady friend? Who is your anonymous eyewitness?'

* * *

Events that transpired after the interrogation session remained blurry and unclear to Zeke. He felt like he had been drugged and lost most of his memories of the recent past.

When he woke up, he found himself inside a hospital room. If he were drugged, the medicine might have muddled up his brain. He just couldn't remember. Did he give his tormentors what they wanted so they let him go? Or did someone rescue him?

Then he remembered Kit, the image of her tied up in a chair with a sack over her head. It sent him into a panicked frenzy.

It was Berta, Mamita's helper, who rushed to his side when she noticed that he was awake.

'What happened? How did I end up here?'

'Don't worry. You are safe now. Somebody rescued you and brought you to the hospital.'

'Who? And where is Kit? There were two of us taken in,' he said again in a worried tone.

Just then, there was a tap on the door and an unexpected visitor entered the room. It was Mr Zultan.

'We miss you already at the office, Zeke,' Zultan chided him gently. 'People were calling, clamouring for an update on the dead boy's story. A human rights group also called, saying they were going to provide additional legal assistance to the boy's family as the case has already been filed in court.'

'A legal case finally filed in court? How long had I been out?' asked Zeke.

'Three days,' Berta answered.

'So how did I get out?'

'Someone bailed you out just in time before you gave them the name of the witness. And someone physically pulled you out from the lion's den. You got some angels watching your back. But I'm not surprised because you're a good man.'

'So, to whom do I owe my life?'

'I'd rather keep you guessing.'

'If it's you, then allow me to thank you.'

'Reserve your gratitude for those who deserve it. The adage "never burn your bridges" still rings true. I'm off, but I'll see you soon,' said Zultan, who turned to leave.

Zeke called out, 'Sir ... '

He had some ruminations running in his mind. His miraculous rescue was already a blessing, giving him a clearer perspective on things. He was given a second life, another chance to make right the wrong, to put things in their proper order including those he couldn't possibly live without.

Like a father, Zultan looked at him, patiently waiting for him to speak.

But Zeke didn't know where to start. 'How do you know ... if it's the right time to ask someone ... What I mean is ... how do you tell someone ... '

Zultan smiled, losing some of his characteristic gruffness. 'Glad you finally came to your senses. Just speak from your heart, and I'm sure she'll know what you really mean.'

* * *

That night, a light knock sounded from the door. It was Kit. She had bought some fruits for Zeke.

'Hey, how are you feeling?' Kit asked. She was only too glad to see Zeke looking better than when she first saw him at the hospital.

'I'm good. Happy to be alive,' Zeke replied.

'I got the ultimate scare of my life when you got abducted,' Kit revealed. 'Can't picture my Friday nights at Conchita's without the ginger ale man.'

Zeke chuckled. 'It was a nightmare. I thought I wouldn't make it out alive … But what scared me most was … when I thought they got you too … which made me realize one thing … '

Kit looked like she was holding her breath, waiting for Zeke to finish.

Just then, they heard another tap on the door. A nurse came in to check Zeke's vitals. There was an awkward silence. Kit sat uneasily on her chair next to Zeke's bedside. She was trying to avoid Zeke's eyes by looking down the floor and then out the window.

When at last they were alone, Zeke continued. 'Remember the time when you would speak up for me in class … '

'Which you hated me for doing,' Kit retorted.

Zeke stopped, bit his lip, trying to compose his thoughts again.

'I'm not very good at this,' he finally said like in a surrender.

'What are you trying to say, Zeke?' Kit asked, her soulful eyes waiting for an answer.

Zeke reached for Kit's hand. 'Marikit Dimalanta, you've been saving my life for as long as I can remember. And many times I wasn't able to show my appreciation and how much I am truly grateful that you're in my life. I realized now that … you are the part of my life I couldn't live without … Will you take me … even if I say the wrong things most the time?'

Kit smiled with tears welling up in her eyes. 'You just said it perfectly.'

Chapter Twenty-five

Friday Night with a Twist

No one's too young to dare the impossible, and no one's too old to do something crazy for the first time.

—Zechariah 'Zeke' Dipasupil

Like never before, Conchita's Bar and Grill flashed a 'Closed to a Private Event' sign and was bustling with music and sounds of cheerful chatter as a hundred guests came together to celebrate the wedding of the owner's grandson, a prominent journalist, with the city's fire chief.

The first- and second-floor dining areas were filled with tables dressed-up with candles and potted succulents. Tiffany chairs were wrapped in purple tulle sashes and mini bouquets. The Zen garden served as the main banquet area and was decorated in theme colours and lights. The guests had a great time dining under the twinkling lights of a thousand light bulbs stringed together and hanging overhead. The kitchen assistants and waiters had been busy refilling the table laden with food.

The wedding entourage was a merry mix of personalities from the seasoned and the prominent, like Benjamin Zultan and Senator Lustro, to the young and the rowdy, like Zeke's colleagues at the newsroom, including Roy and Kit's firefighter associates at the fire department.

The bride looked breathtakingly radiant in an off-white modern Maria Clara-inspired wedding gown with matching strappy pointed-toe pumps. Her hair was held up by pearl-crusted pins, accentuating her heart-shaped face.

The groom, who never liked wearing formal attires, looked dashing in an intricately hand-embroidered *barong tagalog* made from pure piña fibre and paired with pin-striped dark pants and black designer shoes.

He also wore a dark top hat, a pipe, and carried a walking stick for effect. Both groom and bride wanted to depict nineteenth-century Filipinos with a modern twist.

'Tonight, I'm marrying my Friday-night drinking buddy and best friend,' Kit read her wedding vows.

'For thirty-three long years, my heart was on fire and I did not know it,' said Zeke. 'And it took one brave woman to make me realize that she was the reason.'

Zeke drew his bride Kit closer as they sway-danced during their first dance as husband and wife. The guests began to clip Philippine peso bills on their shoulders like a long sash in keeping with the tradition. The money given by guests to the newly weds is believed to bring good luck and prosperity into their married life.

The wedding party lasted until three o'clock in the morning. Zeke and Kit stayed in the garden sipping champagne, talking and laughing. A full moon provided a steady stream of yellow-golden light.

'Who would have expected that we would end up together? I didn't expect you to propose from your hospital bed,' said Kit with a smile.

'You know me. I'm a man of few words. But I also know when it is time to speak up. Welcome home, Mrs Dipasupil,' Zeke chided Kit.

Just then, one of the waiters approached them, saying there was a man outside the restaurant.

'Really, at this hour?' Zeke couldn't believe it.

'Didn't we put a sign outside the restaurant that it's closed for a private event?' asked Kit.

'The man was asking if he can have a word with you in private,' the waiter replied.

'I don't like this,' Kit said. 'Can we just say that it's our wedding night and we want some time alone?'

Zeke asked the waiter again. 'Did the man say what his name was?'

'He says his name is PO1 Gilbert Ryan Guillermo. And he says it's a matter of life and death.'

Hearing those words, Kit had a change of heart. 'The man did not hide the fact that he's a policeman. Maybe it is indeed a matter of life and death. You should go and meet him.'

'But it's our wedding day. We promised we won't go to work today,' said Zeke.

'It's okay,' said Kit. 'You say that news never sleeps. If there's a fire, I'd grab my gear and get on a fire truck in my wedding dress.'

Zeke looked lovingly at his wife, grateful for her brave words that always knocked some sense into him. So, he got up and gave his wife a quick kiss before going with the waiter outside the restaurant to meet the police officer.

* * *

Epilogue

After talking with Zeke, PO1 Gilbert Ryan Guillermo finally found the courage to turn state witness to help shed light on what had really happened the night the boy Eliseo 'Jun-Jun' Reyes, Jr was killed.

Like PO1 Guillermo, the young girl who also witnessed the killing, Yumi Salvacion, was placed under the witness protection programme. She corroborated PO1 Guillermo's statement in court.

As Jun-Jun's case progressed, with the media keeping a close watch on the court proceedings, the court ordered a close-door trial to prevent any trial by publicity. Jun-Jun's case led to a cascade of other drug-related killings to be filed in court, which caught the attention of the International Criminal Court (ICC).

Recognizing the blatant disregard for human life in the indiscriminate killings by police operatives under the government's Oplan Tokhang anti-drug programme, the ICC strongly considered filing criminal cases against President Rodrigo Duterte and those involved in the killings.

The Commission on Human Rights along with other international organizations proposed to bring all drug-related killings to court, with the hope of bringing the guilty behind bars and rendering to the aggrieved families of the victims the justice due to them.

* * *

On nights when he found it difficult to sleep, Zeke would gaze at his wife Kit who lay peacefully asleep next to him. She was gentle as she was fearless. He could not imagine his life without her.

He would think about the boy Jun-Jun, whose cries and pleas were silenced but whose death led to a cascade of events including inquiries, investigations and trials.

He would think about his father, John Alexander, talking in a loud voice, believing that change is possible as long as there are those who refuse to be intimidated.

He would think about his mother, who enjoyed the peace and calm offered by the sea amid the turbulent events in her life.

Like the rising and falling of the tides, there were moments in his life when he couldn't speak even though he wanted to, and those when he wished he had kept his mouth shut.

He was thankful to those who had helped him find his voice and those who had rebuked him when his tongue ran loose.

As an act of giving back to the universe and trusting fully in divine guidance that led him to where he was, he felt nothing could stop him from lending his voice to those who needed it most.

Glossary

Adobo – A popular Filipino dish which involves cooking any meat or vegetable in a marinade made of soy sauce, vinegar, garlic, black pepper and bay leaves.

Aling – Comes from the Tagalog word 'Ale', used to refer to an old woman.

Anak – A local term meaning child.

Ate – A local term meaning older sister. It can also be used to address an older woman who is not a family member as an expression of respect or to connote familiarity.

Bagoong – A salty fermented shrimp paste, commonly used as a dip to add flavour.

Balaeng Hilaw – 'Balae' is a local term used by parents of a couple to address one another, while 'hilaw' refers to a young or unripened fruit. Together, they mean that a relation wasn't official or hadn't fully blossomed as likened to a fruit.

Balut – An unfertilized duck embryo, boiled and eaten with salt and vinegar. It is considered a local delicacy.

Banana que – Fried bananas with caramelized sugar on a stick.

Barako coffee – A variety of local coffee grown in the province of Batangas. The region is famous for its coffee.

Barong Tagalog – Refers to a traditional embroidered long-sleeved shirt for men, used for formal occasions in the Philippines.

Bibingka – A rice cake made from glutinous rice flour baked in a clay pot with live coal on top and underneath.

Chopsuey – A Chinese-style dish made up of stir-fried meat and vegetables.

Ensaymada – A coil-shaped pastry with sugar and margarine on top.

Kuya – A local term meaning 'older brother'. It can also be used to address an older man who is not a family member as an expression of respect or to connote familiarity.

Kwek-kwek – Boiled quail eggs fried in orange-coloured batter.

Leche flan – The Filipino version of crème caramel or caramel custard.

Lechon Kawali – Pan-fried pork belly.

Lola – A local term for grandmother.

Lolo – A local term for grandfather.

Lumban – A third-class municipality in the province of Laguna, known as the embroidery capital of the Philippines because of its beautiful hand-embroidered formal Filipiniana dresses and shirts.

Lumpiang shanghai – Fried pork spring rolls.

Mang – A word that comes from the Tagalog word 'mamâ', referring to an old man.

Maria Clara dress – Refers to an elegant traditional dress for women in the Philippines. It was named after the female protagonist in Jose Rizal's novel *Noli Me Tangere*. It is traditionally made from indigenous materials like piña fibre.

Merienda – A local term meaning 'snack'.

Misa de Gallo – Means 'Rooster's Mass' in Spanish; refers to novena masses held at the break of dawn preceding Christmas.

Oplan 'Tokhang' – The term comes from a combination of two Visayan words 'tuktok' (to knock) and 'hangyo' (to plead or persuade). It is the government's anti-drug operation that was rolled out in 2016 by the Philippine National Police at the start of President Rodrigo Duterte's administration.

Pancit – A noodle dish that originated from Chinese migrants. It is made up of noodles with meat, seafood and vegetables.

Pandesal – A sweet variety of 'salt bread', which is a staple breakfast fare.

Pan de coco – Bread buns with sweet coconut filling.

Pichi-pichi – A tasty dessert made from steamed cassava flour balls mixed with sugar and lye, and topped with cheese or grated coconut.

Poblacion – Comes from a Spanish word meaning 'town', commonly used to refer to the downtown or central area of a city or municipality in the Philippines.

Puto Bumbong – Purple-coloured rice cakes steamed in bamboo tubes called 'bumbong' and popular during the Christmas season.

Santo Niño – Means Holy Child and refers to the Spanish title of the Child Jesus who is widely venerated among Catholics in the Philippines.

Sinaing na tulingan – A common dish in Batangas province made up of mackerel tuna slow-cooked in water with a variety of spices.

Sisig – A local dish made of meat and innards that are boiled, chopped, and served on a sizzling plate with onions and chili peppers.

Suman – Sweet sticky rice wrapped in banana leaves and eaten as a snack.

Taho – A local snack usually peddled on the streets made from warm soft tofu flavoured with caramel syrup.